Thief's Theme: A Love Story

Table of Contents

CHAPTER ONE

Enter the scene as a young man, about six foot five inches with skin so dark that it's almost black, is running through the streets of New York, as he has returned from his trip to London. What business does a young New York male have in London, you may ask? It's simple. Besides tourism and jokes of famous literature (entailing books, plays, and movies), the young man often called Ji had a specific appointment he needed to make. The location? The Tower of London. Why? You may ask. Why would he have an appointment at the Tower of London? Is he a famous celebrity staging a photoshoot? Is he a business man meeting someone there? Or is he a love-struck boyfriend, planning a date with his significant other? None of these are correct, though the last one is the closest. Ji is a thief, and he was in London, more specifically the Tower of London, to steal the Crown Jewels.

Back to the scene, Ji, wearing black construction boots, black jeans, a black button up shirt that is left unbuttoned, and a black undershirt, runs through the streets, with a grin on his face, as several police cars give chase. WOOP! WOOP! Is the sound of the police as the sirens wail loudly, letting all in the vicinity know to clear the path. Fast as he is, Ji isn't superhuman, at least as far as anyone knows, so the cars gain on him quickly and begin to overtake him. Using his cat-like agility, Ji quickly turns the corner down an alleyway only big enough to fit a person or two, blocking the police cars from entering. Still on the run, Ji continues down the alley, past a few garbage cans, and jumps off the wall and over a fence without even losing a step. Keeping pace, Ji then takes a sharp left right into a random apartment building, startling the residents, a young mother and her child. Ji and the mother stare each other down for a moment, both speechless at the unexpected meeting. Ji gulps and then speaks, holding his hands up with palms out.

"I'm harmless, I swear." He says. She looks like she wants to scream but instead she takes a deep breath and nods, likely in fear for her life. Ji shakes his head and continues through the place of residence, jumping through an open window into another apartment to try to lose his tail. "I said I was harmless lady, jeez." He mutters under his breath as he does, annoyed by the mother's reaction. He couldn't blame her however. To her he was just a strange, tall man that had invaded her house. He understood her reaction, even if he didn't like it. Making it through this apartment without incident, Ji jumps through yet another window, straight into a third apartment, further obscuring his trail.

"That should do it." He says aloud to himself. "Only one person would keep chasing me through *that* and at this point, I would welcome her." He muses. "Now let's find my path to freedom." Ji then finds the nearest window and makes his way towards it. With cat-like agility, he flips up and out of the window and up a story to grab a nearby ledge. Utilizing more of his agility, the resident thief kicks off of the wall, jumping up high enough to land on the roof. As he lands he takes a look around, using his hand as a visor to block the sun. First he looks straight ahead and sees a police blockade, complete with about five cars and a group of officers waiting with their guns drawn. "So that way's out." He mutters. He then tries to look to the left. Damn, it's the same thing. He looks to the right, and they have that blocked too. Behind him? He turns and looks and yep, it's the same story. Looks like he's trapped. With a grin he runs his hand through his hair (a high top fade) and exhales. "This should be fun."

With a sudden movement, Ji takes off to his right and leaps from one apartment building roof to the other, soaring through the air like some kind of thieving eagle. He stops for a moment as he lands, to survey the area, which shows him nothing but police blockades as far as the eye can see. He then takes off running once more, this time to the left, and jumps to yet another rooftop. He stops upon landing and looks again, seeing more of the same, and repeats his action, this time jumping forward with the same results. He does this two more times, jumping left and then left again, before realizing that he is truly trapped on all sides. There is no escape. Not here anyway. With a heavy heart, Ji appears to resign himself to defeat and climb down the nearest fire escape. Calmly he walks forward into one of the many police blockades where numerous cars and officers awaited him.

"Alright, alright you win. I'm harmless, see?" He says, walking out with his hands up. The officers don't budge, staring intensely at him as he walks out into broad daylight. One of the higher ranking policemen takes it upon themselves to talk for the group, allowing the others to focus on any sudden movements.

"We all know you're not harmless Merc. Not by any definition of the word." Merc. That's what they called him. It was short for Mercury, the Roman God of Speed, and detailed how he could steal anything at the drop of a hat. The high-ranking policeman keeps his gun trained on Ji as he continues to slowly walk forward. For emphasis, he even cocks his gun, causing Ji to pause for a moment. "You went too far this time Merc. The Crown Jewels? The mother—the Crown Jewels! What were you thinking?!" Admonishes the policeman, likely a sergeant.

"What was I thinking?" Repeats Ji as he continues to walk closer. The sergeant isn't having it.

"Stop right there!" Ji does as he says. "Move another inch, and not only do I fire, but I give everyone here the signal to fire as well." He says harshly. Ji or Merc as they call him just chuckles at the threat as he continues answering the inquiry from before.

"I was thinking...that stealing the Crown Jewels was too good to pass up, clearly." Ji responds with a shrug, as if his answer was the most obvious answer in the world. The sergeant looks incredulous at the reply.

"A-are you serious? Too good to pass up?!" He exclaims.

"Yeah I usually am serious when I speak..." Ji says, though the sergeant ignores him.

"Do you know what you've done? Don't answer that." The sergeant says quickly to cut Ji off as he opens his mouth to retort. "You just went from small time jewel thief and possible bank robber to international criminal. When we lock you up—and we will—you won't be in small time-y jail. You'll be in prison with the big boys. Is that what you wanted? Because that's what you got." Again Ji shrugs.

"I knew it'd happen eventually. No need in being a thief if I wasn't going to be on top. And being on top means going far beyond international criminal, so yeah it's what I wanted." He answers, taking a step forward.

"I said don't move!" Yells the sergeant. Ji grins and licks his lips.

"No, you said to stop! You also said that if I moved another inch, I'd be shot down right where I stand, by you AND all of these fine men and women here." Ji stops to take a look around. "Well I took a step, and I don't see any shooting so." He puts his hands down and starts walking through the blockade towards the police cars. "You know what they say sergeant, you give a man an inch, he takes a mile." Speaks Ji, his back now to the sergeant. The sergeant grits his teeth and swallows.

"I warned you Merc...officers fire at will!" He screams the last part as he pulls the trigger, aiming at Ji's back. CLICK. Did his gun jam or...? CLICK. Nope, it did it again. But how? The sergeant stares at his gun in wonder as nothing but numerous CLICKs are heard throughout the area as every other gun suffers the same fate.

"Kind of hard to shoot a man with no bullets." Exclaims Ji before he does a very acrobatic flip over and around the various police cars, escaping the blockade. "And don't bother chasing me in those. They no longer have any gas...or steering wheels for that matter." What? The policemen all look at their guns in wonder and then to the cars and note that they in fact don't have steering wheels, just as Merc said.

"How?" Asks the Sergeant, mostly to himself. Ji answers him anyway before he takes off running.

"Spoiler alert, I stole them!" He yells as he makes his escape. The police can only look on dumbfounded with nothing they can do to stop him. And so the trek continues as Ji turns down another alley and this time jumps up, kicking off the walls and the fire escape to make his way to the roof. As soon as he lands he hears the sound of a gun cocking as he holds his hands up in surrender.

"Ohiji Olezuo, better known as the thief Mercury, you are under arrest. Again." Says the voice of a young woman he knew very well as she holds a gun to his temple. Ji merely grins at the statement as he continues surrendering.

"Aww, Shar, you used my full name! I'm touched." He exclaims, as he turns to face her. Sharia or Shar as he called her is a woman of normal height with full lips, round cheeks, a small nose, large brown eyes, brown-red hair that is styled into curls, and skin the color of milk chocolate. She wears a pair of black shorts and a dark blue shirt that hug her voluptuous figure, with a black jacket strung over it. On her feet are black sneakers, as she's prepared to run down any criminal. Ji licks his lips as he looks her up and down before he speaks once more. "Now we both know that you don't need the gun, Shar. I'm not going to resist, and you're not going to shoot so..." He trails off, letting her get the picture.

Sharia goes silent for a moment before her expression turns sheepish and she begins apologizing.

"Oh! I'm sorry Ji! I shouldn't have—I had no reason to—that was unwarranted hostility on my part." She explains, stumbling over her words. Ji waves it off.

"Nah you're just doing your job. It's fine." He says nonchalantly. She looks relieved to hear that and gives a breathless smile.

"Yeah...besides it's not like my gun has any bullets in it anyways, knowing you!" She jokes. Instead of smiling with her, Ji raises his eyebrow, questioning her statement.

"Uh...yeah it does. Unless *you* took them out I mean." He states. She looks confused, so he clarifies. "I don't steal from you remember?" It then dawns on her as if a lightbulb just turned on in her head.

"Oh, right. Wait, really? Even in a life and death situation? I mean if I pull that trigger, that's it. You're..." She trails off, not wanting to finish that thought. "I'd almost *want* you to steal from me in that case." Ji returns to grinning when she's done with her words.

"See, that 'almost' is exactly why I don't do it. I know you hate stealing and I could never do that to you." He explains. "Plus I'd be fine. I might not steal from you, but the bullet itself? That's fair game." He says with a cocky grin. Sharia frowns at the implications.

"Ji, you can't steal from a bullet. It's just an object, a projectile, a weapon." She corrects him. Ji appears to be affronted by her assertion.

"Of course you can! What kind of amateur do you take me for?" He says with a hand on his heart. Sharia only shakes her head in disbelief.

"You're delusional Ji." She says as she retrieves her handcuffs. "Anyways, I'm taking you in Merc." Ji's only response is to hold out both of his hands and continue smiling.

"As you wish, mi 'lady."

Ji sits in the back of the police car, silent as he stares at the city. Much to his chagrin he was not put into the back of Sharia's police car, so any hope of conversation or fun is dashed. Instead he stares into the ether, thinking of more things to steal, higher levels of thievery he can reach. He is deep in when his thoughts are interrupted by the officer driving the car.

"OK Merc, let's get a few things clear before we reach the station. First thing's first, where did you put everything man?" Asks the cop in genuine wonderment. Ji looks his way but then looks back towards the window, staring back out into the ether so he can start up his thoughts again. The cop waits a few seconds before realizing that Ji wasn't going to answer.

"OK, don't answer that, it's fine. But tell me, how'd you carry it all out?" Again Ji is silent. "There's over a hundred pieces in that display and ALL of them went missing. There weren't any bags or vehicles with you from what we could see, and we couldn't find any accomplices either. And given you're history, you work alone anyways…so how'd ya do it kid?" Ji maintains his silence.

"OK, then when did you steal it all? Can you at least answer that for me?" This time Ji turns back to the cop and speaks.

"Sure." He brings his fingers together and snaps. "It was in a snap. Just like that." He answers. This causes the cop and his partner to roll their eyes at what they perceived to be an obvious lie.

"If you weren't going to be truthful you might as well stay silent then." Mutters the cop's partner. The other cop, the driver, however has a different idea.

"Come on, Merc. Will you give me *any* information?" Pleads the officer. Ji's mouth forms a small grin at the question.

"Nah. Everything I have to say will be said to Officer Iwuhaki." He clarifies, using Sharia's last name.

"Of course." Mutters both cops in unison.

"Always the same game." Continues the cop's partner.

"Well the drive back to the station ain't short. Anything else you're willing to talk about?" Ask the driver, relenting that he won't be getting any information out of Merc today. Ji shrugs and responds.

"Sure. Sports is cool." The cop's eyes light up, as he finally gets a response.

"OK, Cool. Now we're getting somewhere. Which sport you talking?" Ji shrugs in a noncommittal manner. This annoys the cop but he keeps his cool.

"OK…is football alright?" Again Ji responds with a shrug. "OK Merc, tell me, who's your favorite team?"

"Stealers." Ji answers quickly. "After them it's the Raiders and then the Buccaneers as a close third." The cop sighs and shakes his head, done with Ji's games. His partner takes over for him instead.

"Merc, you know they're not the Stealers but the *Steelers* right? It means something totally different." Ji shrugs.

"Yeah, but it's too good to pass up." He says with grin.

"OK, any favorite players then?" Asks the partner, sure there's not too many stealing puns Ji could make with that question.

"Nah, not really." This answer surprises the partner. How can you be a fan and not have a favorite player. Maybe...

"Oh, do you play then?" Inquires the partner.

"Yeah, on occasion."

"Well what's your favorite position?" Questions the partner further.

"Linebacker clearly." This throws the partner through a loop.

"What? Linebacker? Explain that to me. I thought for sure you'd say Cornerback or Safety or something." The partner says, letting his confusion be known.

"As a Linebacker I get to alternate between stealing the ball in mid-air and stealing it right from the quarterback's hands. Seems like a win-win situation to me." The original cop sighs and steps back in.

"Merc I know you're a thief but seriously. It's not called 'stealing in mid-air', it's an interception. And it's not 'stealing from the quarterback', it's stripping the ball or causing a fumble." Explains the officer. Ji shrugs, not caring for the correction.

"All the same to me." And it was. Stealing was stealing was stealing was stealing. No matter how you dressed it up, in Ji's mind.

"Right." Responds the officer dryly. "Let me guess, in basketball you like defense because you get to steal? In soc—"

"Nah, I like being point guard, assists is my jam." Answers Ji, cutting the officer off. The officer actually stops the car and looks back at Ji with an incredulous look on his face, not believing his answer for a second. "I'm kidding. Not about liking assists, but stealing's definitely my number one. And that goes for all facets of life really." He describes with a grin. The officer just sighs in annoyance and gets back to driving.

"There's no talking to you kid. It's all about stealing." This causes Ji to smile his widest smile yet.

"Now you're getting it!" The cops merely shake their heads and remain silent the rest of the trip. It's about fifteen more minutes of silent travel after that, the cops no longer willing to speak with Ji, and Ji content to let his thoughts wander in the back of the car. Finally they arrive at the station and end the awkward car ride. The cops take him to the interrogation room where Ji's mood brightens up as who else but Sharia is there waiting for him. They sit him down and handcuff him to the table, and leave with a nod to Sharia. Despite them being friends, Sharia is all business and wastes no time getting right to it.

"OK Merc, tell us where the Crown Jewels are! I'm warn—" She's cut off by him simply answering her question.

"Back of your police car. Also the trunk, the passenger's seat, and the hood of your car. It's all there." He explains nonchalantly. Sharia looks taken aback, not expecting THIS level of cooperation and especially not so quickly.

"Really? You expect me to believe that?" Ji nods and smirks.

"Would I lie to you?" She stares at him for a moment before giving the signal (a hand sign) to the people outside the interrogation room to check her car.

"We'll see Merc. My people will be back in a moment to verify your story." She explains. He shrugs.

"Fine with me." She gives him a look and then continues the interrogation.

"OK Merc, tell u—me HOW did you steal it all?" He shrugs again.

"I just did. It's a skill thing really. You wouldn't believe me if I told you." He says.

"Try me." She says forcefully.

"Any time, but do you really want to do it with people watching?" He says with a raised brow, making a rather lewd joke. To his credit, this causes Sharia to blush a bit and become flustered.

"You…not like that! I meant…never mind!" She huffs.

"Hey, you asked. I thought it was strange, you being so forward after all these years, but hey, maybe my charm finally wore you—"

"Enough about your stupid joke Ji. We're moving on." She says with finality.

"Oh, it's Ji now. I like it. And sure, what else do you want to know?"

"Tell us when you stole the Crown Jewels." She demands.

"Us?" He questions with a brow raised. He continues nonetheless. "I told the other guy that one, the guy whose car I rode in? It was in a snap." He says as he snaps with his finger. She stares him down with scrutiny, but he just looks back with a smile.

"Even if we were to believe you, a 'snap' is not a time. That's a time period." She states. He shrugs and remains silent, beckoning her to continue. "In other words, you're telling us how fast you did it. We don't care about that. We want to know at what time did you commit the crime?" Again he shrugs. She's surprised he doesn't get tired of doing that.

"It was broad daylight, I didn't really look at a clock, so I can't help you with that. If I could, I would." He explains. She stares at him once more, trying to read him and determines that he is in fact telling the truth.

"OK Merc, that's it for now. Stay here." She commands as she exits the room.

"Aw man, it's back to 'Merc' again?" He complains as she closes the door. After that outburst, Ji waits patiently in the room for another hour before he's collected by two officers he's never seen before. The officers take him away to a temporary jail cell, a holding cell until he can be transferred to a prison. He looks around as he's being walked away and sees Sharia walking into an office, likely to fill out the paper work related to this case. He directs a smile her way as he's lead off.

Ji waits in the jail cell, daydreaming about stealing more and more things, letting his imagination go wild. Maybe he'd steal something big time like another national treasure, or better yet a global treasure. And why stop there? Why not go higher and higher until he reached the ether with his stealing? There was no limit for a true thief and he intended to prove it. Ji continues to think and dream until he realizes that Sharia has likely gone home for the day given how much time has passed. He pouts a bit at her not even visiting him as she leaves, but shakes it off as he has work to do. There's an officer keeping watch over him at the moment, but that shouldn't be that big of a deal. One blink should be enough to...

Sure enough the officer blinks and suddenly the bars in the jail cell are gone. The officer rubs his eyes to make sure he's seeing correctly.

"What the—?" He looks on with disbelief as now the entire cell is gone. He looks down to get his gun and looks back up and is now in a desolate area. The entire police station is now gone. Stolen by the world's greatest thief.

CHAPTER TWO

Two small children sit together in the open field section of the park, where there's green for as far as the eye can see and even a small creek for children to play in. The first of the two children is a little boy with black cornrowed hair, dark brown skin, a red shirt with childish designs, and white and black sneakers. The second of the two children is a little girl with red-brown hair done up in pig tails, a blue dress with a white belt, and white shoes. The two children are resting, visibly breathing hard from playing one of their many games together. The little girl is the first to speak in between her breaths.

"Not...fair...Ji...you're...too...fast." She manages to get out, pouting a bit as she does. Ji gives a small grin at the compliment before responding.

"No one ever catches me!" He exclaims loudly. He then looks over her pouting form. "You're...pretty fast too." He says, breathing less than her and thus only pausing once in his speech to gain some air. This brightens her mood some.

"Really?" She asks, unsure of the statement.

"Yeah, no one ever catches me, but you got this close!" He says, putting his pointer finger and his thumb only an inch away from each other, nodding in reassurance as he does. She smiles and responds.

"I did? Next time I'm gonna catch you for sure!" She exclaims, having gotten most of her breath back. He nods silently, not wanting to disagree with his new friend but not able to consent to simply losing.

"You ready for another game?" He asks, looking over at her. She nods.

"Yeah let's go!" She says as she gets up from her seated position. At the moment, Ji remembers the gift he got for his newest friend. He'd been meeting her in the park for some time now and wanted to make sure she liked him, so he got her a gift.

"Wait, I got you this." He says, holding out a piece of candy he stole earlier. Her eyes widen and lighten up when she sees.

"Thank You!" She says as she takes the candy and hugs him, causing him to blush. For the rest of the day, Ji was distracted, only thinking about the thanks that the candy got him.

A few years later the same two children are again at the same field in the same park. This time the boy child has an afro and is significantly taller than the girl child. The boy child is also wearing something different, blue jeans, sneakers, and a black t-shirt. The girl child now has long braided hair and is wearing a purple shirt-skirt combination with dark purple shoes. The two sit down on the grass next to each other, hanging out as they take in the beautiful view that the park provides. This time the boy child is the first to speak.

"Shar…" He begins, trailing off as he prepares himself for some difficult words.

"Yeah?" She asks, looking at him as he speaks. He swallows and tries again.

"Shar, have you ever seen anything at like a store and said to yourself, 'I want that?'" He asks timidly and hesitantly. She looks confused but answers.

"Yeah, all the time. Why?" He takes a deep breath and then clarifies.

"OK, not like 'I want that', but more like 'that should be mine', like…you know stealing it?" He asks quietly. Sharia almost barks out a laugh as she playfully hits him on the arm.

"Of course not silly. I don't like stealing." He remains quiet, unable to speak without feeling bad or putting his foot in his mouth. All the time he eyes a necklace he got her a few months back. It was sparkling in the sunlight and was a beautiful shade of red that matched her hair. It likely wasn't real diamonds or anything, but still it was pretty enough that he had to get it. He had to give it to her. He wanted her to thank him as she had for the candy he gave her those few years ago and nearly every day after. He wanted her to thank him as she had for little random toys he used to steal for her. Her hug, her smile, those were what he craved. At least in the beginning. Now, there was something else to it.

Several more years pass and now both children are in middle school, meeting at the park on a weekend when class is out. The boy child is tall now, nearly the size of a normal man in height, though he's very skinny and still identifiable as a young child. He wears a blue hoody with black jeans and black and white sneakers, and his hair is even larger and puffier than before, still in the shape of an afro. The girl child has grown as well. She's a little shorter than the average woman in height, and has yet to truly fill out though she was budding. Her attire was a simple red shirt with butterfly designs and tight black jeans with dark red sandals. She also wore two bracelets on her left wrist, one on her right, and the necklace she received so long ago, and her hair was now puffy in the shape of an afro as his was. Again the two are hanging out and again the boy child breaks the silence.

"So Shar, you don't like stealing right? You hate it?" He asks, still looking ahead at the sky and the view. She looks at him quizzically and answers.

"Hate's a strong word, but yeah I guess my feelings of dislike for stealing are strong too. Why? Where are you going with this?" She asks, suspicious of his conversation.

"So then you'd mind if the things I gave you were stolen. Angry probably?" He says in almost a whisper. She has to lean in to hear what he says, before she visibly recoils in shock and a bit of disgust.

"What!?" She asks, alarmed at his words as she holds her necklace with an iron grip. Hesitantly she asks her next question. "Is that what your gifts were Ji? What they are? Stolen Property? Illegal...objects that belong to other people?" He sighs and looks her way now, having dreaded this conversation for a long time.

"So I take that as a yes then." He says simply, reading her outrage. "I take it you don't want any more gifts from me either." He speaks in a deflated, almost depressed tone.

"No, I don't." She replies in a stern manner. Subconsciously she looks down at her bracelets and wonders if she should take them off. Ji notices.

"Don't worry about the stuff you've already got. It's…it's good. You won't get in trouble for it. I made sure of it." He says quietly, looking down. She sees his sadness and lightens up a bit.

"That's not the point Ohiji." She talks with a softened tone. "But thank you." She finishes as they both sit there in silence, looking down and contemplating what just happened. For Ji, he knew she'd look at him differently from now on and for Sharia, well she didn't know what to think at the moment. Ji was still her best friend and a good person as far as she knew, but he was also a thief, something she hated. It's Sharia who breaks the silence this time.

"I meant what I said Ji. No more gifts, not if they're stolen. I can't…I just can't." She states. Ji only nods and remains silent. The silence remains for the rest of the time they're at the park.

Days later Ji is walking around in a black hoody with black pants and black boots, scouting out the area near the biggest bank in the city. He takes note of all the cameras as well as the guards and their shifts. More importantly he notices the small things, the nearly nonexistent moments of vulnerability, the openings he can exploit. Ji had been craving this for some time now and had subtly been watching the bank for months, even as he stole from other stores: food from grocery stores, necklaces, rings, watches, and bracelets from jewelry stores, and damn near everything from department stores, he always kept an eye on the bank.

By now he's learned the traps they had, the combinations to their safes, and how much time he has to be in and out before anyone saw him. And if an alarm is rang, he knows how much time he had before the cops would come too. Nothing is left to chance. It's tough, but he's a thief and proud of it. He'd be damned if he's stopped just because of some security or the size of his target. His blood boils in excitement and his heart pounds just thinking about the thrill, about the accomplishment he would soon hold. It was good to get this out now as he'll have to be completely calm and extremely silent when it all went down. He knew from experience. That night he suits up with a black shirt, grey jeans, and black running shoes and is on his way. He reaches the entrance of the bank, takes deep breath and goes in.

Sneaking quietly through the bank, Ji escapes from the back room and the safe, with copious amounts of money in hand. He'd already disposed of the marked bills inside of the bank and now just had to avoid the cameras and the guards on the way out. His excitement almost surfaces as he takes one step to many around a corner, only to see a guard still making his rounds. Calming back down, Ji steps back and waits for the guard to pass before promptly exiting the bank with his score in his hands.

As Ji exits the bank and gets to his safe spot, he can't help but to smile, completely happy with his accomplishment. This was big, this was huge! He can't wait to tell...oh right. His mood completely deflates as he remembers that his best friend hates stealing. She wouldn't celebrate with him; she'd just berate him and scold him. While she'd never turn him in, she'd make him feel bad about it, like he was scum for doing it. He didn't need that right now. He then smiles again. At least he can brag about it to his other friends, J.R., Marshon, and Bruce. And maybe a few of the prettier girls too. Girls love bad boys after all. Now to get them to believe him...

A couple of years later, Ji and Sharia, now both in high school, both sit down at the park, next to each other. It's been so long that they've now dubbed this 'their spot' and are again hanging out on the weekends when class is out. Ji has cornrowed hair, the first signs of a mustache, a red button up shirt, black jeans, and black construction boots on and is easily a head taller than Sharia if not more. Sharia has filled out and has on a black skirt with a blue top, and black boots. Her hair is still styled in the form of an afro. This time it is Sharia who breaks the silence.

"Ji." She starts, getting his attention as he was staring off into the distance, likely daydreaming about further thievery.

"Huh? Yeah?" He says, a bit startled as his trance is disturbed.

"How would you feel if you worked your whole life for something? If you dreamed to one day have something? You work at it, and you work at it, and you work at it, and finally after all that hard work, you got it?" She asks. He looks at her with a bewildered stare, thinking the question to be odd, but regardless he answers her.

"I'd be happy of course." He answers truthfully, allowing her to continue.

"Now imagine some thug, some brute taking all of that away from you. All of your blood, sweat, and tears just snatched from you. You're left with nothing, not even your former feelings of happiness." She speaks with a cold and pointed tone, clearly trying to make a point. A point Ji understands, nodding as she speaks.

"Look I get it, but I don't steal from people, just establishments, stores, businesses–"

"Banks?" She inquires, cutting him off. He pauses for a moment, caught off guard, telling her all she needs to know. "Yeah I know it's you Ji. Everything's been you hasn't it? All of these strings of robberies that the cops can't figure out? The stores, the banks, the…" She trails off, going silent for a moment, looking down and shaking her head. "I…I'm disappointed really. I thought you were better than that." She finishes.

'Better than that?' Thinks Ji. 'Oh great, she thinks I'm a lowlife then.' He takes a small breath and speaks after letting the silence reign for about a minute.

"So…we cool still?" He asks, testing dangerous waters. At his words, Sharia looks at him sharply in scrutiny but nods nonetheless.

"We're still friends Ji, I just...don't support your thievery. And one day...I'm going to put a stop to it. Mark my words." She exclaims. He looks at her questioningly. 'Is she going to tell? Or does she mean something else?' He wonders. He continues to wonder for a long time, unable to bring himself to voice his thoughts and ask her.

More time passes and both Ji and Sharia have graduated from high school. Despite that, the two still meet in their spot, hanging out as they always have. Ji now has short hair with waves brushed into it, a mustache and beard combination, and has on a black jacket with a white shirt underneath as well as black pants and black white construction boots. Sharia now has her afro split into two separate puffs and is wearing a white and black dress with white flats on her feet. Her wrists no longer bear the bracelets Ji gave her, but the necklace remains. As she did last time, Sharia breaks the silence.

"I have good news Ji." She says, catching his attention.

"Hm?"

"Your days of thievery are over!" She conveys excitedly.

"Really?" He asks amused by her declaration. "And why is that?" He inquires. She smiles at the question and answers enthusiastically.

"Because I've just been enrolled into the police academy!" She replies. Ji can only stare at her in shock. Internally he is upset, very upset and it all starts to dawn on him. 'She wouldn't...S-She did! So this is what she meant by putting a stop to it?'

"That's right, soon officer Sharia will be on the case. And I WILL catch you Ji. Bet." She declares with a smile on her face. He nods silently, still thinking. 'How can we remain friends like this?' He wonders. 'Won't she be hounding me at all times?' Sharia seems to read his thoughts as she answers his internal questions, looking at him softly.

"Big dummy, we'll still be friends. It's just when it's time to work, we're on opposite sides." She explains. He nods and then lets a grin form on his face.

"Sounds like fun." He says.

"Hmm?" She almost questions.

"What?" He asks, unsure of why she made that sound.

"Oh I just didn't know you liked losing so much." She states with a playful smile. 'What?' He thinks. 'Oh...oh! She's saying she's going to catch me all the time! Well...probably.'

"It's not the end result Shar, but the chase." He replies with a smile. "Besides who could resist being arrested by such beautiful specimen?" This causes her to blush and smack his arm.

"Flattery will get you nowhere thief." He laughs at her proclamation.

"You say that now..." He trails off, mischief filling his mind as he gets a sparkle in his eye. "Thinking on it, I need to get back to work. I owe you a celebratory gift for getting into the police academy." He speaks, with a grin, the irony of the situation not lost on him. Sharia responds to the set up just as he planned.

"Oh you! You better not! No stolen gifts, remember?" She retorts, flustered by the idea. Ji shrugs and waves it off.

"I remember." He states. 'But what I do with the stolen money however...' He thinks with a sinister internal grin.

CHAPTER THREE

Ji waits for her at their spot in the park with a wide grin on his face, knowing this would be a spectacle to behold. He knows that by now, word has spread about his latest conquest and Sharia would be looking for him, to give him a piece of her mind. Rather than run and increase her stress levels and thus her frustration and levels of ire she held towards him, he decides to pick a spot that she can and will easily find and make things easier on both of them.

Sure enough, it only takes her an hour to find him. And considering that the park is about thirty-five minutes away from the police station, she made pretty good time. Ji can tell by the force behind her feet and the way she marches up to him that she's angry. This only causes his grin to widen and her frustration to grow. As she reaches him, she glares at him angrily and basically growls her next words.

"What did you do?" She commands. To avoid her full wrath, Ji reins in his grin and manages to put on a straight face…only to shrug at her question.

"I'm sorry Shar, you're going to have to be more specific. I've done a lot of things." He explains in an innocent tone. Her glare intensifies.

"You know what I mean. What did you *just* do?" She demands.

"You mean escaping from jail? I mean you knew it was going to happen. You may be able to catch me, but no structure can hold me. We both know that." He points out.

"No not that! I mean yes that, but not the escaping part." She tries to clarify unsuccessfully.

"Shar you got to be more straight with me, I'm not sure what you're talking about." He says with a shrug.

"The police station you dummy!" She yells, causing him to flinch a bit. "As soon as I get home I get a call about some...tall tale of you stealing not only the bars of your jail cell, not only the full cell, but the entire police station! Now I'm not sure what everyone's smoking, but they're sure it's you. So whatever you did, reverse it and put the police station back!" She instructs him. In response, Ji puts his hands up in surrender and grins once more.

"And if I don't? You going to arrest me officer?" He asks in a taunting manner, clearly amused by the situation.

"Yes I am! And wipe that stupid grin off of your face!" She commands as she takes out her cuffs and steps towards him. Ji complies and helps her put his hands behind his back.

"Fine with me, I'll just escape like always." He replies.

"And I'll continue to catch you like always." She retorts as she finishes putting the cuffs on and begins hauling him to her police car. This only causes him to smile.

"It's a date." He says as she continues hauling him off to her car.

"So where are you going to take me exactly, with no police station and no jail cell?" He asks innocently. This causes Sharia to pause as he had a point. "And how can I return the police station if I'm all tied up and restrained? You got to compromise here Shar." She acknowledges his pleas and roughly takes the cuffs off as she huffs in anger at being defeated so easily.

"Fine, you're right. I'll let you go for now, but you have to promise to return the police station and reverse...whatever it is you did within an hour. Ji raises his eyebrow.

"In an hour?" He questions. "Do you know how large a police station is?" This causes her to glare at him again.

"You're asking someone who works in the police station that question?" He concedes the point to her internally. "Story says you stole it in less, so make do, or I'm coming for you." That statement causes Ji to raise both eyebrows.

"Wow, first you're trying to force me into your car for some alone time and now you're coming for me. Why Sharia Iwuhaki, if I didn't know any better, I'd say you were trying to flirt with me." He says with a smirk. Sharia blushes at the implications and hits his arm.

"Get your mind out of the gutter, Ji!" She says, only causing his smirk to transform into a smile. "And remember, return the police station or you're done!" She says as she gets in her car. He shrugs.

"Alright, will do!" He says, waving goodbye she starts her car and begins driving off. "That was fun. Now...what's next on the list...?" He ponders to himself.

The next morning, Sharia wakes up feeling as if something is wrong. She looks over at her phone and sees over a dozen messages waiting for her and sighs while rubbing her temples. Ji's definitely been up to something again. Carefully she listens to each message, noting that the sounds of panic increase with each one. After about five minutes, she's finally done and...she doesn't really know what to make of it. Silently she turns on the news and sees the exact thing that's baffling her: '7 Wonders of the World, stolen!' is the headline as newscasters and experts talk endlessly at the different possibilities of what's happened. Somehow, just like the police chief, just like the international authorities, the newscasters and the experts all agree that this can only be one man: the thief known as Mercury.

"Oh Ji, what have you done?" She questions aloud as she shakes her head. "Why is it I always have to clean up after you?" She mutters as she quickly freshens up, gets dressed, eats, and makes her way to the police station. 'That's right, the police station.' She thinks. 'You better have come through on your promise Ji or I'll...' her thoughts trail off before they can get too vicious. It doesn't take her too long to speed to her place of work and when she does, she breathes out a sigh of relief. The building is back and Ji kept his promise.

"At least he's good for one thing." She mutters as she exits her car and quickly makes her way into and through the police station to the chief. He notices her as soon as she steps through the door and quickly runs to her, looking ragged and tired.

"Oh thank god, Officer Iwuhaki, you're here!" He exclaims with pure joy in his eyes. This causes every cop in the station to stop what they're doing, turn around and cheer much like he did. Sharia blushes a bit at all the attention, but manages to gather herself and get to business.

"That I am chief. What's the situation?" She asks, knowing the gist, but wanting the details.

"Have you seen the news?" He questions. Sharia nods, gesturing for him to carry on. "Well, to be honest with you, that's pretty much all we have." Sharia looks at him confused a she responds.

"Wait, we have the same information that *the news* has? So we have nothing?" She asks, bewildered. The chief grimaces and nods.

"Pretty much. Even the higher ups all have the same information: one moment the Seven Wonders of the World are there, and then the next moment they're not." He explains.

"Wait, all of them? At the same time?" She inquires, still incredulous at such a thing. He nods again.

"That's what sources say."

"And we think Merc did this?" She asks with scrutiny. He shrugs and scratches his head.

"Yeah pretty much. I mean...who else could?" He asks.

"I get that, but that's never been enough to start a manhunt before! We have no proof!" She argues, trying to get some semblance of normalcy back in her life.

"We've never had a situation like this before officer! Besides, we're not asking you to execute him! We just...we need you to find him as no one else ever has. Ask him about it; get him to put them *back* like he did the police station. Fix this." He says.

"And if it's not him?" She questions.

"Then it's worse than we thought and we're all screwed." He speaks, causing her to look at him in confusion. He continues to speak, clarifying. "We know that Merc is somewhat reasonable, at least when you're involved. If it's someone else...well they're a complete wildcard with impossible abilities that we can't hope to compete against. Let's just hope for all of our sake, that this is Merc. And let's be honest, we know it is." States the chief. Sharia nods.

"Right. Where do I start chief?" She ponders aloud. He sighs and rubs his head.

"Normally I'd say where your gut tells you, but the people are going crazy and need some kind of...assurance." He describes. Sharia's heart drops.

"And I'm that assurance." She states dryly. The chief winks and points a finger-gun at hers.

"You got it! The one person to ever catch Merc is on the job, so don't worry, we got this! That's basically what you're conveying to them."

"Even if we *don't* got it?" She asks, not wanting to lie to people like that.

"*Especially* if we don't got it." He says as he pats her on the shoulder. "Go get 'em girl. I know you can do this." She nods silently and takes a deep breath, ready to begin her trip around the world.

"When do I leave?"

Sharia exits the plane, groggy from her nap. She's cross right now, angry at Ji for forcing her to go through all of this. 'I got you a free trip around the world' he'd likely say, and then she'd punch him in the face, slam him on the ground and arrest him after a few kicks to the ribs. At least that's what she's fantasizing right now. 'Stupid Ji, with your stealing fetish.'

"Who steals the Pyramids of Giza?" She questions as she enters the country of Egypt. She looks up and notices the distinct lack of Pyramids in the distance and her mouth falls open as she gapes at the impossibility she's witnessing. "My god, he really stole them. They're…gone." She says under her breath in amazement. "How do I comfort anyone about this?" She wonders to herself. Quickly she makes her way to the authorities in Egypt, mentally readying herself for her meeting about the missing pyramids.

About an hour through said meeting, Sharia is ready to bash her own brains out, the hard way on the glass table in front of her if she has to. These people knew nothing and had just spent the last hour spit-balling and complaining, with nothing productive being done. Having had enough, she clears her throat and interferes.

"So let me get this straight!" She yells loudly, above the chatter, causing everyone to look at her. "No one saw Merc enter or leave the country?" She asks. As people look to open their mouths, she gives them a stern look that says 'either nod or shake your head'. They comply and shake their heads. "OK, and no one saw *how* the pyramids were taken?" Again they shake their heads. She closes her eyes and rubs her temples before pointing to an Arabic man with glasses on his face and a short beard. He wasn't anyone special as far as she knows; she just needs someone to clarify. "You! Tell me what we *do* know."

He nods and clears his throat, clearly terrified and intimidated by Sharia. He does eventually gather enough courage to speak.

"All we know is that one minute, the Great Pyramids are there, with people on side of them, and even inside of them, taking tours…" He trails off.

"And?" She asks, beckoning him to continue. He nods and gathers his courage once more.

"And the next minute, they're gone. As if it were an act of God." He explains, looking up and pointing at the ceiling as he does.

"OK, got it, so one minute they're there, and next minute they're gone. We have no confirmation that Merc was even in the country and...you know what never mind. Thank you for your cooperation gentleman, we got it from here." She speaks, starting out frustrated, but ending her statement politely.

The men all get up and bow slightly at her, making sure to shake her hand.

"Thank you Miss. Please, catch this man and bring him to justice!" Is the message she gets from all of them, more or less. 'I'll catch him for sure, but bringing him to justice? Not so sure on that one.' She thinks, remembering all the times she's caught Ji or 'Merc' as they know him, but also remembering that he escaped each time. She takes out her phone and look at the next item on her list. She has to resist the urge to facepalm and smack herself on the head as the next meeting is in this same building, but about the Lighthouse of Alexandria, another of the Seven Wonders, also located in Egypt.

'Why wouldn't they just discuss that in the same meeting?' She wonders, frustrated at having to go through yet another meeting with the same people about the same fruitless topic. 'From now on, I'm checking my phone ahead of time and bringing up every freaking wonder the country has before leaving the meeting.' She promises herself as she turns right around and walks back into the building.

Another hour and another meeting is complete with virtually the same information as before. Just like with the Pyramids, no one has seen Ji or 'Merc' in the country, no one has seen him leave, no one saw exactly how the Lighthouse was stolen, and the Lighthouse too just disappeared out of nowhere in seemingly a second flat. Sighing in frustration, Sharia swears revenge on Ji. 'When I get my hands on you...' She thinks as an evil smile finds its way on her face. She then exits the building and is immediately on a plane to Iraq.

"Next up, the Hanging Gardens." She says to herself as she settles into her first class seat. "At least I get to fly first class." She mutters as she drifts off to sleep, trying to sleep off some of the stress. Two hours later she arrives and is ready to tackle another useless meeting that exists only to reassure the people that the thief (Ji in this case) would be caught. Breathing hard she steps off the plane and looks at her phone.

"Good." She says to herself. "Only one Wonder here and thus only one meeting." She then finds her way to a taxi and is on her way to the building where said meeting is. It takes another thirty minutes, but she does finally arrive at the building, about ten minutes early for her meeting.

"Here goes nothing." She says as she exits the taxi. "Wish me luck." She says to no one in particular as she heads in to try to survive yet another meeting on this debacle. An hour later, she's feeling about half as frustrated as before. She paid less attention than she did in the first two meetings, knowing it to be gibberish, but from what she could gather, it was the same situation. No one knew anything.

"OK, so no one saw the thief or how he stole the…" She pauses to look down at her phone. "Hanging Gardens? And the Gardens just…disappeared, correct?" She asks in a bored tone, stifling a yawn in the middle of the last sentence.

"Yes, Miss that is correct." Speaks on of the members of the meeting. She yawns again and gives him the same answer as before. Well, virtually the same answer.

"Alright, thanks for this…riveting meeting and the information. We got it from here. Trust me, I'm an expert on J—Merc." She says, waving off their concerns as she walks away and out of the building. 'Another complete waste of time.' She thinks. 'Oh well, time to go to…' She looks at her phone. 'Turkey. There's two Wonders missing there, the Temple of Artemis and the Mausoleum at Halicarnassus. Joy.' She thinks as she walks wearily to a taxi and takes a ride to the nearest airport.

Another hour, another flight, and another nap for Sharia as she arrives in Turkey for yet another meeting. Well it's supposed to be two meetings, but hell if she's going through that again. This time she was going to bring up *both* wonders in the same meeting, no matter what anyone else said. But first she needed to get there...

After hailing a taxi and getting to the correct place, Sharia only has a minute or so before the meeting starts. Being who she is, she simply walks in to the place and sits down, not bothered with the stares. This time Sharia waits for only twenty minutes before intervening.

"OK, men we've heard much of the same before. You haven't seen the thief in or out of the country and the Wonder just suddenly disappeared, the..." She glances down at her phone. "Temple of Artemis. Now tell me about the Mausoleum at Halicarnassus." She inquires, struggling to pronounce the name. The men look speechless as she asks. She waits for a full minute in silence before one of the men clears his throat and responds.

"Um...Miss, we were only here to discuss the Temple. The next meeting is for the—" She doesn't allow him to finish.

"I know the details sir, but *that* is a waste of time. You want us to help you as soon as possible? Make all the details available as soon as possible. Now tell me, what happened at the Mausoleum?" She commands with authority. The men are hesitant, but soon fall in line and begin speaking about the second Wonder as they spoke about the first. Sharia knows the information is useless and likely the same as before, but she does sit back and let them speak, nodding occasionally to make them feel better about themselves. After thirty more minutes, she cuts them off.

"I see. Thank you men for your input. We got it from here." She says as she abruptly gets up from her seat and leaves the building. Before she knows it, she's on an hour flight to Greece to discuss the last two Wonders. 'And after that, it's home sweet home.' She thinks with a smile as she dozes off for a quick nap.

In Greece, it's the same deal. She arrives at the meeting, they give her nothing, she forces them to talk about the second wonder, and still no real information. The only thing different is the amount of time she allowed them to talk (about ten minutes per wonder) and her leaving statement.

"Thank you men, it's been enlightening. We'll be in touch." Not allowing any force to stop her, Sharia quickly hops onto a plane to make it back to New York and back to her home, more importantly her comfy bed. She falls out as soon as she hits the mattress with one thought on her mind. 'Ji, you're dead.'

A grin adorns Ji's face as he knows Sharia is back in town and out for his head. He knows about the various trips she went on because of him as well as the mind-numbing meetings she had to go through. It was because of this that Ji isn't at their normal spot in the park. No, Ji is on the run, moving constantly around town, making it a challenge to get him. He doesn't exactly want to face Sharia right now, and even though he knows deep down inside that he's making it worse by leading her on a chase, some part of him didn't care. It was like a game…

"Hello, Mr. Olezuo?" Came the voice of death cutting off his thoughts, using a sweet tone to mask her true emotions. 'Damn, she got me.' Thinks Ji as his grin turns more to a nervous smile. He looks around and remembers that he's on a train to the other side of town, part of his whole 'constant movement' plan that in hindsight was more stationary than he wanted. There was no escape.

"Uh…hey Miss? What can I do for you?" He asks, playing along to hopefully lessen the punishment. To her credit, Sharia, now wearing her curls in a ponytail and dressed in a black shirt pink shorts combination, as well as some glasses (for her disguise?) merely smiled and responded.

"Well you see, I have this *difficult* and *unbelievable* project I need help with and I was wondering if you could come with me and take a look?" She asks with a bright smile. But Ji could read between the lines. Her smile said 'come or die' or 'come or I snap your neck' or something of that nature. So he could do nothing but resign himself to fate and go with her.

"All Seven Wonders Ji? ALL SEVEN WONDERS!? How do you even— What goes through your mind when you plan these things?" She asks, clearly peeved at him. He responds with a Cheshire smile.

"Pretty Impressive huh? I think it's my greatest work yet." He says, with in a proud tone.

"That's an understatement." She mutters underneath her breath.

"So officer, are you here to arrest me?" He asks, innocently but holding out his hands. She sighs and puts the cuffs on.

"Sure I guess. Though I'm not sure what's the point anymore." She says in a dejected tone. "Come on, you're going to straight to State prison due to your last debacle. You've proven...too dangerous for jail." She informs him. He shrugs.

"Good with me." He responds. 'Why do I even bother?' She wonders as she puts him in her car and takes off to the prison. She drops him off after making sure he registers and goes through the proper processes, though she leaves before he has to strip, blushing a bright red when she realizes what part he was going through. Ji only winks at her when she leaves, but she surely doesn't see it, too consumed by other thoughts. Within the hour he's in his cell, in a prison jumpsuit, staring at the bars as he daydreams about further more things to steal.

"What even comes after the Seven Wonders of the World? Is there anything left?" He wonders aloud to himself. He then shakes his head. "Of course there is! What am I saying? I just have to get creative!" He says to himself as he gets up and stretches. "Man, I'm bored." He then grins and remembers exactly who he is: the world's greatest thief. Boredom isn't an option.

An hour later a guard walks by his cell, wanting to check up on the one and only Merc, to make sure that...he was still there basically. As the guard comes upon his cell he sees Ji in normal clothes (a black jacket with a white button up shirt and black jeans), playing some kind of game system right next to a computer, a laptop, and what looks like half-eaten lobster.

"What the hell?" The guard exclaims, rightfully confused. "Where did you get that?" He demands.

"Stole it." Answers Ji, not looking away from the game. "Lobster's not as good as I thought it'd be. It's so expensive and yet so mediocre." He continues, as if expecting the guard to agree with him. The guard does agree with him internally, but he knows that this can't continue, no matter how right the thief is.

"Well that's too bad, because I'm confiscating all of it." Declares the guard. Ji just shrugs.

"Alright, just wait until I beat this level— welp, just did. You're good to go!" He says happily. The guard looks at him wearily as he grabs the stuff and starts taking it with him, his hands obviously too full.

"You're on thin ice Merc. Do this again and we'll take you to solitary." He warns. Ji shrugs, not really caring where they take him. No cell could hold him after all. Now how long should he wait until he takes everything back?

It's only the next day when he steals everything back, this time eating crab cakes instead of lobster. The guard walks by again and has to rub his eyes to make sure he's not hallucinating.

"Wha—? How? Where'd you get this stuff?" He asks again.

"Stole it. Just like last time." Answers Ji, surfing the web on his laptop. The guard almost blows his top.

"That's it! You're going to solitary!" States the guard in anger. Ji looks up at him and shrugs.

"OK. Will you let me have my stuff in solitary or…?"

It's been four days since Ji was taken to solitary confinement. And each day he would be in his own cell, wearing his own clothes, playing games, surfing the web, and eating good food. Each day he would be caught as the guards would check on why he wasn't eating their food and drinking the water provided, and each day they'd confiscate everything only for him to steal it away. After the third day, Ji decides to steal something more esoteric, like the ability to see his stuff, making it invisible to the guards. From then on he hasn't been bothered and simply enjoys the simple prison life.

On the sixth day of solitary, Ji is finally 'let out' of the cell...and into an interrogation room by two cops. The first cop jacks Ji up by the shoulders and tries to intimidate him.

"OK Merc, here's how it works. We ask you a question and you answer it. If you don't..." He glances to his partner who cracks his knuckles. Ji merely yawns, causing the cop to slam him against the wall, hard and the other to hit him with a gut punch. Ji laughs and lets them in on his secret.

"I don't feel pain, so hit me as much as you want. I stole that from myself a long time ago." He says through a grin.

"What kind of gibberish are you speaking Merc? We didn't hit you *that* hard. Not yet." Says the first cop, confused at Ji's words. "Now, here come the questions." Ji shrugs, not caring either way.

"OK punk, how'd you steal it? How does some punk like you take the Seven Wonders of the World?" Asks the second cop. Ji shrugs.

"I just did." THWACK. He's punched across the face. True to his word, he doesn't feel the pain however so it's all lost on him.

"Where are they!? Where'd you put them punk?" Yells the second cop, ready to strike again.

"My secret storage place." Answers Ji. THUD. He's hit with a gut punch that he simply laughs off.

"Where is that?" Asks the first cop. "Be straight with me." Ji instead grins as he answers defiantly.

"Not telling." Says Ji in sing-song voice.

"Look here you little punk!" Says the second cop as he tries to make it to Ji.

"Whoops." Says Ji as the cop somehow finds the cuffs on him rather than Ji. The second cop looks on in bewilderment as the first cop moves to restrain the thief, only for him to disappear.

"Where did he go?" Asks the first cop.

"I don't know! How'd he get these cuffs on me?" Asks the second cop.

"Dammit! We got to call this in!" Says the first cop as he looks for the key to the cuffs, but can't find it, likely because Ji stole it. Mass panic ensues as the police issue a full lockdown and city-wide search for Merc, a wanted global criminal who just escaped. Traffic is stopped as every vehicle is searched, legal or not. Stores are turned over, apartments are raided, and the street is filled with every able-bodied officer, all looking for the world's greatest thief. All within a couple of hours. Finally, someone has the sense to call Sharia who walks into the cell to see the two cops, trying to break the second cop free from his handcuffs, banging them with a hammer. They succeed just as she walks in, shaking her head in embarrassment.

"Officer Ihuwaki! Thank god you're here! We had Merc in here, interrogating him about the theft of the Seven Wonders." Starts the first cop.

"And then the kid just attacks us out of nowhere, like a rabid dog!" Says the second cop.

"He's always so peaceful ya know, so we weren't prepared for that." Continues the first cop.

"So the kid got away." Finishes the second cop. Sharia looks at them with disbelief.

"You're saying that Merc attacked you guys?" Both men look at each other and nod.

"Yeah, dude went crazy on us! We're lucky to be alive!" Says the first cop. Sharia doesn't look impressed.

"Somehow I don't believe you." She says, arms crossed. "Now, where have you searched exactly, to declare him missing?" She inquires.

"Well right now, the chief has every vehicle, every house, every apartment, and every street corner being searched to find the bastard." Explains the second cop. Sharia raises her eyebrow.

"He does? That's excessive. And stupid. If Merc truly escaped, such a search wouldn't help us. Now has any one searched his cell?" The cops open their mouths and close them again.

"Uh…no. But we searched the rest of the prison, we swear!" The first cop exclaims. Sharia pinches her nose in frustration.

"Come on, let's look at his cell." She says as she starts walking to his assigned cell. She stops when the cops don't follow her. "Come on, what are you waiting for?" She asks, annoyed.

"Well um…that's not his cell anymore." Explains the second cop. Sharia looks confused.

"What do you mean that's not his cell anymore? Was he moved?" She questions.

"Kind of." Says the first cop. "He was transferred to solitary, gave a guard some trouble from what I heard." He informs her.

"Solitary?" She yells, her eyes bugging. "What could he possibly do to be confined to solitary?" She asks, internally worried for her friend and what treatment he might be getting. The cops shrug.

"Not sure, but I've never questioned the guards before. Wasn't going to start for that punk." Says the second cop. Sharia sighs and rubs her temples.

"OK, let's go to solitary then." The cops nod and they move on their way. Quickly the find solitary and open the door to Ji's cell. Sure enough there he is, eating pizza and watching a huge ninety inch HD television. As his door opens up he waves happily to Sharia and continues watching TV. Sharia sees him and her mouth drops open. 'I completely understand.' She thinks to herself, answering what he could've done to deserve solitary confinement. She shakes her head and goes to speak when the cops do first.

"That's it punk!" Says the first cop.

"You're going to get it!" Finishes the second cop, both ready to charge forward and lay a beating on Ji. Sharia stops them however by holding up her hand.

"I'll take it from here officers." She says, staring down Ji as she does. He finishes swallowing his piece of pizza and grins at her, giving her a thumbs up. Yeah he's going to get it. The cops barely rein in their fury but hesitantly nod, allowing Sharia to take the reins. She is the expert on Merc after all. Sharia closes her eyes for a moment and then snaps them open. It's time to get to work.

CHAPTER FOUR

Ji and Sharia sit across from each other in the interrogation room, silent as Sharia stares him down, trying to figure out how to get him to talk. 'Let's try the basics first.' She thinks to herself.

"OK Merc, tell me, how'd you steal the wonders?" She asks, looking him in the eye for any trace of trickery as he answers. Ji shrugs.

"Like I told the last guy, I just did." He answers.

"I'm going to need more than that Merc." She says, trying to coax the answer out of him.

"Look, it's a really basic and simple thing. I stole them how I'd steal anything else. I located them and I took them. Simple as." He explains with a sincere tone. She narrows her eyes.

"I don't believe you." She says. He shrugs.

"I know that you wouldn't, that's why I answered the way I did. Any more questions?" He asks.

"Same ones as before." She says, causing him to sigh in annoyance.

"Well that sucks. I already answered these before, and answering them again is just boring. How about I ask some questions of my own?" He inquires. Sharia scrutinizes him, looking for any kind of ulterior motive. She doesn't find one.

"Sure Merc. If it makes you talk, you can ask anything you want." She relents.

"Alright then. So Shar…how've you been? Anything interesting happen in your life, besides me?" He asks. The basic simplicity of his question causes her to sigh.

"I've been good J—Merc. And no, you're pretty much dominating my life as it is." She states.

"Good to know." He responds with a toothy grin, liking that he was dominating her life so much.

"Now, answer my question. Where did you put the Seven Wonders?" She probes.

"And like I said before, I put them in my secret storage place." He repeats.

"OK, where's your secret storage place located? How do we reach it?" She asks? Ji shrugs.

"You don't really. I couldn't really tell you where it is, I'd have to show you. I can do that right now if you'll let me." He replies with a wide smile. Sharia stops and thinks about it hard. Knowing where his secret place was would help, but if it's just her and him, she can't really recover the wonders.

"Not now." She begins. "After the interrogation."

"I don't know officer, I might not be up to it after the interrogation." He stops, leans forward and looks her in the eyes, staring deep into her soul. "I'm not going to say it's a one-time offer, but it's rare. So choose wisely Shar." He advises with a sagely tone. She thinks on it again, her heart telling her to go as it's something she REALLY wants to see, the secret lair of the world's greatest thief. It'd provide so much insight on how to truly stop him and find the things that he takes. Then again, if he was willing to show her, then it likely wouldn't affect him much at all. Even more, she couldn't guarantee—No, she knew for a fact that he wouldn't allow himself to be brought right back to the interrogation room afterwards and she didn't feel like going through the effort of catching him again.

"I'll pass." She speaks with finality. Ji shrugs.

"Alright, it's your choice." He says. "A bad choice, but ultimately yours to make. Now, my turn to ask a question." Sharia nods, giving him permission.

"Go ahead." This causes him to grin, almost making her wish she hadn't said that.

"You been working out?" He suddenly asks, as if they were having casual conversation. This confuses her.

"What? No! No more than usual at least." She answers truthfully. Ji shrugs off her answer.

"Hey, I couldn't tell. I was thinking you *must* be working out because...well you look good Shar. Anyone ever tell you that?" This causes her to blush, though she does gather her composure.

"Now's not the time Merc." She says, brushing off the compliment. This doesn't stop him from talking.

"Hey you want to go get dinner?" He starts. "I think we're overdue for some hanging out time." He speaks almost absentmindedly. Sharia rolls her eyes at his statement and takes a deep breath before steeling her eyes over and slamming her hand hard on the table.

"Enough games, Merc. What's it going to take to get the wonders back?" She questions intensely. Ji stares her down before answering.

"Just ask." He says with a shrug. This throws Sharia throw a loop. All this hard work, all of this locking him up and going through interrogation and they just had to *ask*? No, it couldn't be this simple.

"What? All we had to do was ask?" She voices her disbelief. Ji shakes his head.

"No, all *you* had to do was ask. Ask, and you shall receive." He informs her. She looks at him with a raised brow before an idea comes to her head.

"I suppose I can't ask for you to stay locked up and not escape?" He shrugs again.

"You can, but I probably won't give you that. Anything else, but not that." He answers truthfully. 'Damn, it was worth a shot.' She thinks, though she's sure that deep down inside she'd want him to truly be locked up forever. It just didn't sit right with her. Then again she knows he'd be alright and just steal anything he needed and bring the necessities to his cell, so she probably shouldn't be worried. Getting off of that train of thought, she turns back to the issue at hand, getting the Wonders back.

"Fine. The Wonders, put them back." She demands in a harsh tone. Ji smiles and snaps his fingers.

"I wouldn't call that *asking* exactly, but it'll do. Your wish is my command." He says. Sharia looks at him wearily as if expecting him to do something else.

"You don't expect me to believe..." She trails off, not finishing her statement. Ji nods to answer her question.

"I do actually." She sighs and leaves the room to make a quick call to the chief to see if somehow Ji had actually put the Wonders back. It didn't make sense, but nothing around him did anymore.

"Hello Chief?" She asks, making sure she got him.

"Sharia! My best girl! I heard about how you found Merc for us, again. And I just want to thank you for everything—"

"Thanks Chief, but that's not what I'm calling about." She says, cutting him off.

"Oh, right. Of course. What is it that you need?" She hesitates, not wanting to sound completely insane, but there was no way to say this otherwise so...

"Well I spoke with Merc and he says he put the Wonders back." She informs the chief.

"While in his cell?" Questions the chief, surprised.

"In the interrogation room, yes. I know it sounds crazy, but can you check to see if they're in fact back in place?"

"...yeah sure. Give me a second." He says as he puts her on hold. Sharia takes this time to look back at Ji who had a confident grin on his face. 'He better not be messing with me.' She thinks as she waits. 'This will be really embarrassing if he is.' Another ten seconds of silence and the chief comes back.

"Well...uh...I don't know how to say this but...the Wonders are back. Looks like Merc told the truth...somehow." Sharia's mouth involuntarily transforms itself into a smile.

"Thank you chief, that's all I needed to know." She says.

"No problem." He responds as they end the call. Sharia then takes a few moments to compose herself and wipe the smile off of her face. She couldn't afford to go back in the room like that. Not against Ji. She needed to be all business and no play, and bring back her serious attitude. She does just that as she walks back in the room with a stern look, slamming her hands on the table as she confronts Ji about what just happened.

"I don't know how you did it, or what you're doing, but I *will* find out." She warns him. He just grins back at her. Damn, he was unshakeable. "Besides that though, thank you." She says as her expression softens. It immediately hardens again as she continues. "Now, back to your cell and try to remain there. At least until I've left for a good while at least. We don't need them getting ideas." She commands. Ji fake salutes her.

"Aye aye captain. I'll make sure to come find you for dinner when I'm out."

"You're too much." She grunts under her breath in frustration as she beelines it out of the prison. A day later, Ji escapes, returning the games, TV, laptop, and computer that he took.

A day after that, Sharia finds herself walking around town trying to think of how to stop Ji or 'Merc' for good. He's her friend yes, but he's also on the wrong side of the law.

"You can stop me by having dinner with me." He says, interrupting her thoughts. She turns around when she hears his voice, cuffs ready for the arrest.

"You!" She exclaims as she actually tries to arrest him on the spot.

"I can see you're not up to it right now." He says as he disappears from sight, causing her to double take and look around for his possible escape route. 'What did he just do?' She wonders. She manages to shake it off and return home, her little trip for air and thinking on how to take Ji down was done. No way she can go back when he's bound to just interrupt her like that. When she gets home, a surprise is waiting for her: a table set with food.

"Oh god, they're going to make me an accomplice after seeing this." She states aloud, holding her head in her hands, looking stressed over the situation.

"Relax." Ji says, lifting her face by her chin, looking her in the eyes. "Eat." She blushes at both the contact and their proximity and gently pushes his hand off of her chin. She looks down at the food and realizes that she'll be in trouble whether she eats it or not.

"Might as well." She breathes out with a shrug as she digs in to the food.

"That's the spirit!" He exclaims as he too sits down with her and begins feasting. The two eat together, talking as they do. Ji waits for her to eat a few dishes before he starts asking questions.

"So, mi' lady, is everything up to par and to your liking." She looks up from her meal and nods slowly.

"Yeah, except for the part where it's stolen. You know I hate stealing." She reminds him once more.

"I do, you've told me over and over again. And yet here we are: the world's greatest thief and someone who hates stealing, good friends, hanging out and having dinner."

"And being cuffed." She says as she cuffs him to the table stealthily, looking at him with a smile that says 'Gotcha!' He merely raises an eyebrow and beckons her to look down. She does and she sees that somehow the cuff is off. When did he?

"Nice try, but not today." He starts. "At least wait until my next masterpiece." He says as he waves his hand over the table as if presenting something. "Dessert?" He inquires. She goes to say no, trying to decline anymore stolen food, but as she looks down she notices that various desserts have appeared on the table. "I got your favorites, from bakeries all around the world." This causes her heart to flutter somewhat.

"F-for me?" She questions rhetorically, stuttering as she does due to the excitement and unexpectedness of the situation.

"Of course. A special gesture for a special woman." He says silkily. She blushes at the compliment and instead chooses to look down and keep eating rather than respond. Ji shakes his head in wonderment as he too begins eating, making sure to pick the desserts she wasn't eyeing at the moment. Another five minutes and both are done, allowing Sharia to finally look up from the table and say her piece.

"I may not like what you do Ji, but the thought is still...thank you." She says sincerely. He grins in response.

"Any time, anything, anywhere." He says with a wink as he disappears before her eyes, taking the dirty dishes and any evidence of their meal with him. Sharia sighs now that it's over, but can't help but to smile at his antics and at his words. He may be a thief, but he was still not only her friend, but a good person at heart.

CHAPTER FIVE

The next morning Sharia wakes up and she can already tell something is wrong. She takes a look at her phone and...yep, twelve messages, definitely another heist from Ji. She sighs and turns on the television to see exactly how far he's gone this time. The answer makes her jaw drop and her eyes bulge. "Las Vegas Gone!" Reads the headlines as the same experts from before discuss their false logistics and far-fetched theories on who did this and how Merc did it. Come to think of it, how is Merc doing this? One doesn't just steal an entire city. It's not possible. And yet...here they are, scrambling to make sense out of that exact situation. Sharia rubs her temples to relieve the building stress. 'Why couldn't he be a simple thief?' She wonders as she knows what she must do. She must find Ji and bring him to justice. Again.

Ji runs through the streets of New York, donned in a red jacket with a black shirt underneath, black jeans, and black and red construction boots, having the time of his life as the police chase him, trying futilely to bring him in for questioning about Las Vegas' disappearance.

"Stop!" Screams one of the chasing officers as he reaches for his gun. The officer looks down when he feels nothing there and realizes that his gun is gone.

"What's the matter? Cat got your gun?" Asks Ji as he grins and continues his escape, taunting the officer. Other officers try to help, having just got into the picture, but find that their guns are gone as well.

"Hehehehe!" Cackles Ji sinisterly as he revels in their confusion. Just then a police car rides up, gaining speed with its siren going. WHOOP.WHOOP. Comes the familiar sound as Ji looks back and sees his old friend, the police car, behind him. This time he manages to keep his distance on the car, as impossible as it seems, and soon has an entire squadron of cars chasing him. With a quick juke, Ji turns into traffic, making it more difficult for the cars to follow his much smaller figure. Ji makes several acrobatic maneuvers in a row, first jumping up and on top of the roof of a speeding car, then flipping off of it onto the road, then no-hands cartwheeling over a truck and running up the front of an eighteen-wheeler going the opposite direction, lying back on the roof and catching a ride. The police cars try to no avail to keep up, but once he performs his superhuman feats of agility and lands on the eighteen-wheeler, they know they're beat. At least for now.

Ji rides the eighteen-wheeler for another few streets before rolling off of the roof and landing on his feet, opting to take a stroll through New York at a leisure pace and take in the sights. 'Hey, ain't I near J.R.'s house?' He thinks to himself as he looks around at the street names. 'I am. Let's hang with him for a sec.' He says as he turns left and travels to his newest destination, his friend J.R.'s house.

It only takes Ji about ten minutes to reach J.R.'s house even at such a leisure pace, but by the time he gets there, he still manages to be bored out of his mind. KNOCK.KNOCK. KNOCK. He raps on the door, hoping his friend J.R. is actually home today. He hears some commotion inside the house and then after a few seconds, the door opens, revealing who else, but J.R. himself, a stocky black man with somewhat blown out hair, a mustache, and nothing on but a undershirt tank top and some shorts.

"Ji? Is that you?" Asks J.R. in a deep voice. Ji just grins and holds his arms out to his sides.

"Who else would it be fam?" He replies.

"Oh snap, that is you! Damn, son how've you been?" Asks J.R. genuinely surprised to see his friend.

"I've been good. You know, me, stay thieving on my 'Merc' game." Answers Ji, a joyful smile still on his face. He steps forward and the two do a special handshake, one they developed as kids as Ji steps into his house.

"Ah, so that's you then? Stealing them artifacts and what? Las Vegas now?" Questions J.R. as they sit down on a worn couch that sits in front of a decent sized TV with a game system in front of it.

"You know it. They don't call me the "World's Greatest Thief" for nothing." Brags Ji.

"Damn, that's tight. You always been on that Aladdin stuff. But you ain't bring no heat here right?" J.R. asks, looking around to make sure no cops are around. Ji waves him off.

"Nah man, I wouldn't do that to you. It's why you haven't seen me in a while, been too busy stealing. The heat on me's ridiculous when they can catch me, but I'm clear right now. Plus they know better than to involve my friends or family." Ji responds as he picks up a game controller. "And Aladdin don't got nothing on me B'. He don't get down how I get down, nah mean." J.R. nods as he turns on the game.

"Yeah I get you. Can't believe you got Five-O scared of you like that though. That kind of coverage extend to the feds too?" J.R. questions without taking his eye off the television as the game turns on. Ji shrugs.

"Not sure yet, but I'm sure somebody's told 'em by now. And if they don't know, they will soon." He says as he too watches the screen intently, both preparing themselves for the game. "I'm international now baby, and deadlier than ever." He states as he reaches over and fist bumps J.R.

"Preach." Is all J.R. says as the two engage in a riveting battle of video games.

Ji stays for a good three hours playing video games before he says goodbye to his friend J.R. and heads back out. When he does, he notices men in black suits following behind him but keeping their distance. He also spots some all black cars and vans tailing from even further back, trying to be stealthy about it. Speaking of the feds, here they were, and it looks like he'd have to lose them too. He just hopes that they know the rules.

Ji continues walking aimlessly, not having a real destination in mind, and wanting to test how far these special agents following him will go. He walks for hours, covering the entire city, and manages to lose the men and half of the cars, but the vans were still going. He also notices a helicopter flying above that passes by every so often, about once an hour, and knows that that too belongs to them. So they were persistent to say the least, but they didn't seem to be interested in stopping him or taking him in, only in watching them. With a grin on his face, Ji knows what he has to do: show them that you can't watch 'Merc' if he doesn't want you to. Suddenly Ji disappears from their sight, causing a minor panic as their cameras, radars, and scanners can't find any trace of him.

"Find him dammit!" Ji can hear over the ear pieces as he stands behind the helicopter pilot, unseen. "No man just disappears out of thin air like that!" Leaning against the interior of the helicopter with a smile, Ji waits for a good ten minutes as pandemonium occurs. The helicopters try flying through the city several times, as agents and vehicles cover the ground, while snipers cover the in-between. Of course none of them find him, which simply amuses Ji to no end. With a quick sleight of hand, Ji then takes their camera footage they have of him and all the files, all the information they got on him, even in their databases. In their stead he leaves a simple message: "Merc was here."

Ji descends from the helicopter and starts his trek back home for some rest, as it'd been a long and eventful day. WHOOP. WHOOP. Comes the sound of the police brigade, their vigor renewed after some down time in their search for him. Rolling his eyes in annoyance, Ji merely steals their cars from out under them and continues on his way home, shaking his head.

"First you take their guns, then you take their cars, and then...their women." He says to himself, in a theatrical voice. He walks a few more blocks, getting closer to home when some...special looking men come up to him, dressed in strange black robes come up to him. Keepers.

"Thief!" Begins the first of the two men, both speaking in distorted voices.

"Mercury as they call you. You have messed with the natural balance, and continue to every day that you live!" Adds on the second of the two men.

"Breaking limits you shouldn't!" States the first man.

"Stealing the impossible!" Exclaims the second man.

"You are to cease and desist!" Says both men in unison as they throw strange looking chains at Ji's person. The chains are pitch black with white outlines, as if energy is radiating off of them and wrap around Ji's body in less than a second, before he can think, constricting him and not allowing movement. Not one to let himself be trapped, Ji quickly disappears along with said chains, leaving the men empty handed.

"Track him!" Yells the first man. The second man looks at the back of his left hand and then at the palm before throwing his hand down in frustration.

"I can't. Nothing is picking up a signal, it's like he's disappeared from this realm!" Conveys the second man.

"Or he's stolen his ability to be perceived, to be tracked." Theorizes the first man in robes.

Ji stops to chill at where else but his and Sharia's special place at the park. He takes in the view, staring into the distance at the peaceful setting.

"Looks like it's starting to get real." He looks around and sees Sharia wearing her hair in braids with a dark blue jacket on over a black shirt and dark blue shorts. "And now she's here. Great." He mutters to himself as he turns to face her.

"Ji, I got a lot of questions for you and you're *going* to answer them. At the prison. I'm taking you in." Ji smiles at her confidence and her words but is almost forced to shake his head no.

"I'll let you take me in later." He starts as he looks around. "But right now, some heavy stuff is going down." He explains as her expression changes from one of determination to one of confusion.

"Ji what are you—" She begins to question, but he cuts her off.

"I need you to lay low Shar, because some powerful men, strange men are after me."

"Who?" She asks, wondering if it's perhaps the CIA, FBI, or some other government agency.

"The Keepers." He says. "They think I've broken too many rules, gone too far with my stealing." He informs her. "So give me a minute or so. After I'm done with them, you can take me in." Sharia is still confused and voices her confusion.

"How do you—?" She tries to ask, but he cuts her off again to her annoyance.

"Stole the information." Ji responds, tapping his head.

"That doesn't make any sense!" She exclaims. One can't just steal information after all. Especially not directly into their heads. Life didn't work like that.

The two Keepers are still in the same area Ji left them in, unable to track Ji and his whereabouts. The two do converse about the information they have on him however.

"So this thief, was he born with special abilities or powers?" Asks the first Keeper.

"No sir. He just has the innate skill to steal anything. Technically nothing he does is supernatural, it just seems so." Explains the second Keeper. The first Keeper looks distraught at this news.

"Damn, that makes this much harder. If it were supernatural...any leads?" He asks, trailing off from his previous thoughts.

"Her." Says the second Keeper, bringing up a picture of Sharia on the back of his palm. "Sharia Ihuwaki, a childhood friend who always manages to capture him. He does escape however whenever she leaves. Should we procure her and use her as bait?"

"No." Says the first Keeper, waving his hand. "If anything we should actually use her for what she's worth, recruit her to our side, and let her catch him for us. Angering a thief of this caliber would be foolish and deadly." He explains.

"Right sir." Says the second Keeper with a nod. "Tracking her location now."

Meanwhile, Ji and Sharia stand across from each other at the park, Ji waiting patiently for what he knows is to come and Sharia simply confused about it all.

"OK Ji, you said to give you a minute, but how long are we going to just wait here for something to—" She's cut off from her scolding as fifty men with strange black robes appear from nowhere, surrounding Ji and cutting off her line of sight to him. Ji immediately holds his hands up.

"I don't fight, I steal. So please leave me alone." He states. "I'll return Vegas…eventually." He ends with a grin. Sharia almost facepalms at Ji's still playful attitude in a situation that seems so serious. The Keepers, to their credit don't react much to the joke.

"Not acceptable, Ohiji Olezuo, you're coming with us." States one of the Keepers, the first man from before. Ji shrugs.

"I beg to differ but OK." He says as in a moment every Keeper drops to the floor. Sharia's eyes widen in alarm.

"What did you *do*?" She asks, worried.

"Steal their consciousness." He answers with a shrug, putting his hands down. This only makes things worse.

"What? This isn't making any sense Ohiji." Sharia exclaims.

"Don't worry, you'll understand in due time." Says Ji in a sagely tone. "Now you were going to arrest me?" Sharia looks unsure, her eyes somewhat gravitating towards the weird robed men on the ground.

"Are you sure it's OK? She ponders. "Those men aren't after you?" He gives her a confident smile.

"I'm sure." Is all he says as he allows Sharia to slap on the handcuffs and take him to prison.

The two arrive at the prison but are immediately stopped by a black van sitting in front of the prison that cuts Sharia's car off. Men in black suits swiftly exit the van and open the doors to Sharia's car as they explain the situation to her.

"Officer Ihuwaki, we're CIA. We're taking 'Merc' here to a special government prison to get this thing sorted out. You're welcome to join him, if you wish." Speaks one of the men. With all that's happened today, Sharia has no words and simply nods, riding in the back of the van with Ji as both are blindfolded for secrecy reasons. Well, she's blindfolded. Ji has a bag put over his head.

It's another hour before they reach the facility, and when they do, both are hurried out of the van, grabbed by their arms, and led into a special room: the interrogation room. They sit Ji down in the room and lead Sharia to a separate spot of the prison.

"If we need you, we'll call for you Miss Ihuwaki. For now, let us handle this." 'You won't get anything out of him!' She wants to yell, but she doesn't have the energy. She knows they'll be back once Ji doesn't cooperate, but for now she finally has some time to think over just what the hell is happening with Ji and those strange men and him stealing...things that can't be stolen. It all threw her for a loop.

As Sharia ponders previous situations, Ji is going through a current one. The agents in the room are prepared to perform a full scale torture session to get him to return Vegas to its rightful place. The first agent to try, a man with wide shoulders and no facial hair, walks into the room with a cold aura about himself.

"Mercury, the world's greatest thief, the one who stole the Seven Wonders of the World. And now, you've stolen Las Vegas. Unlike the police, we don't care how you did it, we don't care when you did it, or where you're holding it. We simply want Las Vegas back where it belongs. Give us that, and we *don't* have to start pulling finger nails." He informs Ji in a serious tone. Ji merely shrugs and utters four words.

"Not going to happen." Oh how he loves antagonizing people, especially authority figures who try to 'interrogate him'. Unlike the policemen from before, the agent doesn't lose his cool. He simply stares Ji down and says two words of his own.

"I see." As he leaves the room. He returns not a minute later with what Ji knows (after stealing the information from his mind) to be a finger-nail pulling torture device. "Remember Merc, you chose this." Laments the agent as if he actually cares. He moves closer, ready to place the device on Ji's right pointer finger when suddenly the cuffs on Ji fly off and onto his hands instead, making him drop the device. The agent looks down at his cuffed hands in surprise and then back up at the now-uncuffed Ji. He realizes the danger and backs out of the room. Ji just grins and taunts the man.

"Welp, that was easy. Who's next?"

Dozens of agents try to get Ji to crack, each attempting different methods. One tries waterboarding, but Ji simply disappears right before the water hits and then reappears right next to the agent commenting as he shrugs.

"I don't like getting wet."

Another agent ties him up to a chair with chains, cuffs, and ropes, and swings a hammer at his kneecaps, stopping a centimeter too early to try to scare him. Finally, after five swings and Ji unwavering from his position, he swings seriously, only to find himself in the chair somehow and Ji free, holding the hammer, twirling it in the air. Other agents try to hit Ji, but he simply disappears before they can connect. Others try more classified forms of torture, but each time he simply leaves or puts them in his place before anything can happen. Finally, after an hour, the agents know they're beat and retrieve Sharia from her room. By now Sharia has come to terms with what happened earlier and is no longer silent or flustered. She walks into the room with a purpose and immediately gets settled and starts the interrogation.

"Look, I'm not sure exactly what's happening with those men and somehow Vegas going missing but...you've had your fun right? Return Vegas and do your thing already Ji." She commands him in a serious tone, whispering his name so others don't hear it. He nods in understanding.

"Now how could I resist such a pretty face?" He says softly as he leans forward to whisper in her ear. "It's done." This causes Sharia to blush, but she hold it in and nods, looking back at the CIA agents.

"Go check agents, you'll see that Vegas is back in its rightful place." She states, now confident that Ji won't lie to her in a situation like this. The agents scramble to find proof, some getting on the phone, others looking up pictures on a satellite, and some checking other surveillance equipment. It takes a minute or so, but they all come to the same conclusion: Vegas is back.

"OK now—" She turns to speak, but notices that Ji is gone. She shakes her head and gets up, leaving the interrogation room. As soon as she does, the agent in charge walks up to her and offers her a handshake (which she takes) and thanks her.

"Thank you for your services Officer Ihuwaki. We couldn't have done it with you." He praises her truthfully. Sharia gives him a small smile, knowing his words to be true, but not wanting to say much in fear of sounding prideful or arrogant. Instead she nods and continues walking, only to be stopped by another agent. Sharia is stopped by what seems like a thousand agents, all thanking her for helping them return Las Vegas, before she finally reaches her destination: Ji's assigned cell.

She stops at the cell, seeing the expected sight of Ji chilling inside with everything he needs to be comfortable, and walks up to the bars.

"Bye Ji." She says softly, causing him to look her way and walk up to the bars as well, touching his fingers to her through the openings.

"Hope to see you soon." He says with a smile. She smiles as well before turning to leave the facility. Sharia panics for a second as she realizes that she doesn't know where she is, but the feeling is quelled by the sight of a black van and an agent waiting for her, to escort her back to her car. This time the ride is made sans the blindfold out of respect for her efforts.

Ji waits an hour after she leaves to escape, disappearing in plain sight, though Sharia has a different experience at the same time. Having had a long day, Sharia is glad to be home and steps out of her car and opens the door to her house, ready to jump into bed. As she steps in, she sees two of those strange men with the black robes, Keepers, as Ji called them, waiting for her. These men are different though as their robes are more...decorative than before with more symbols on them. Before she can figure out what to do, one of the two men speaks, greeting her with his distorted voice.

"Hello Miss Ihuwaki, have a seat."

CHAPTER SIX

Sharia's adrenaline begins rushing as she tries to figure out what to do. The men seem to sense her discomfort and try to assure her.

"Relax Miss Iwuhaki, we're not going to hurt you." States the man who hasn't spoken yet. Sharia doesn't care to hear their attempt at calming words.

"How'd you get in my house?" She asks, more concerned with her security and well-being.

"We are very powerful people, Miss Iwuhaki, Keepers of Order, above the police or even the government." Speaks the first man, pacing about.

"We've noticed your skill, Miss Iwuhaki." States the other man. "Especially with handling 'Merc' also known as Ohiji Olezuo. This is why we want you to work with us, to be on our team." Sharia, is surprised by the offer, still on edge at strange men being in her house.

"Just like that?" She questions in a suspicious tone.

"Just like that." Answers the second man. "As you saw earlier, we can't do anything to capture this 'Merc', but you can. Maybe one day we can even work together to keep him contained once you capture him and turn him in." He explains. Sharia's head spins from the current development, but she understands enough to know that this is something she'd normally be interested in.

"Um...ok." Sharia starts. "Should I quit my other job? Is there some type of transfer protocol?" She questions, unsure of how to make the transition from cop to...Keeper.

"No need." Says the first man. "You'll still work for them officially, but behind closed doors, you will truly work with us, as a Keeper. As for pay, we'll provide you a stipend every month, and we'll give anything else you need on the job in the first week." Continues the first man.

"Sharia, you won't *only* be taking cases with him, but they will be the majority of your cases as you're the only one who can…" Explains the second man, trailing off at the end.

"I understand." Answers Sharia, nodding to in acceptance.

"Good." Speaks the first man. "Well then, have a good day, Miss Iwuhaki." The men say as the walk past her and out the door, nodding to her as they leave. She smiles in response.

"Thank you." She says, nodding back. Once the men leave and have been gone for a few seconds, Sharia slumps against the now closed door, frightened and terrified at the men who just left her house and the situation that just transpired. "Ji, what have you gotten yourself into?" She wonders aloud.

The next few days pass without much fanfare, as the weekend hits and Sharia prepares a movie night for herself, where she watches a few movies of her choice and feasts on snacks, while wearing only her pajamas (an undershirt and a pair of pink pajama bottoms). Of course she can't be so lucky to have that day to herself as just when she's prepared to hop on her couch, bowl of chips with salsa and dip in hand (among other snacks), who else is sitting there but Ji, also donned in an undershirt and pajama pants (but his are blue).

"Hey girl." He says in a pseudo-seductive tone. Sharia just rolls her eyes, not even shocked or surprised that he's here since he's done this so often, and sits down next to him. As soon as she does, she thinks back to the men who were in her house, the Keepers, and becomes worried once again, taking a deep breath as she calms herself down. This causes Ji to raise his eyebrow, but she soon brushes aside the feelings and speaks.

"Hey, you staying for movie night?" She asks.

"Of course, I wouldn't miss a chance to spend time with my girl! You know outside of being arrested and interrogated and all that good stuff." Again she rolls her eyes. As if any of those things counted as spending time together. And he didn't have the right to complain considering it's his choice of…career that gets them into these situations in the first place. Well that and her dislike of said career…wait did he say?

"I'm not your girl." She states nonchalantly. Ji becomes flustered at the statement and tries to recover.

"I meant girl…like I would call my other friends my boys. Yeah…that." He says, words stumbling out of his mouth. Sharia looks at him with scrutiny and even chuckles a bit.

"You're a bad liar." This causes him to grin.

"It's why I try not to lie to you." He states truthfully. "Now come sit next to poppa so we can watch the movie." He says while wagging his eyebrows. She sighs but obeys, sitting right next to him under the covers as they watch an action-adventure flick. The movie has a lot of fighting scenes, so both Ji and Sharia enjoy it, and there's also a sci-fi element that for him and a romantic subplot for her to fawn over. Overall it's pretty good, about as good as a movie about a kung-fu space cowboy can be, and Ji makes his enjoyment known.

"Wow that was a good one! What's next on the list?" He asks. Sharia smirks and holds up a romance movie. Ji's expression changes immediately to one of disgust. "A chick flick? Ugh, why do chicks always want to watch those? Why can't we watch something fun?" He complains.

"We just did." She says. "That was your choice, and this is mine." She says as she gets up briefly to replace the movie.

"Fine." Replies Ji in a defeated tone. Sharia takes great joy in this and even sticks her tongue out at him in a childish manner as he crawls back in the covers, causing him to lick his lips subconsciously. The two friends watch this movie as well, Ji just staring at the screen patiently, not moving or doing much, and Sharia doing all sorts of things. First she somehow moves closer and ends up snuggled up to Ji, not that he's complaining, and then she ends up crying at some of the more so-called touching moments. He just rolls his eyes at the display, but knows he can do nothing but let it pass and wait for the movie to be over. Finally it does end and the credits roll, allowing Sharia's thoughts to wander once more to the Keepers and the situation that happened earlier in the week. This time she decides to speak on them.

"Hey Ji, those men, the Keepers…" She begins, trying to explain.

"Yeah I know. You don't have to say it." He assures her.

"I want to." Confesses Sharia, wanting to get it off her chest so she doesn't feel scared or guilty anymore. "They wanted me to join them so I could capture you like I always do. These men…they sound dangerous. What are you into?" She inquires, fearing for his safety.

"You." He answers simply, causing her to blush and hit his arm.

"Not that! I mean, what is this business with these men? What do they want?" She probes. Ji shrugs in response.

"Justice probably. Or some warped form of it. Think of them like…advanced cops or whatever. It's nothing to worry about." He reassures her as he yawns, feeling sleepy. "I always escape." He points out, making her feel better as he does truly always seem to escape, no matter how bad or impossible the situation is. The two soon fall asleep together, resting peacefully in each other's arms.

Sharia is the first to wake up, smiling as she does, liking the warmth of being so close to Ji and the feeling of being in his arms, though she'll never admit it. She looks up at him worried, putting her hand to his head, wondering if he'll be OK. Ji wakes up and grabs her hand, startling her, as he answers her thoughts out loud.

"Of course I'll be. You'll be there." He says with a grin as he kisses her hand. It's too early to blush so Sharia simply watches him do it as he continues to speak. "So, you fixing breakfast or should I?" He questions with a grin.

"Neither." She responds, sitting up and out of his arms. "You need to go. Wanted fugitive and enemy of the state and every form of law remember?" She says referring to him.

"Right, right." He says waving it off. "Alright then, this was fun. Let's do it again." He says, yawning. "Some time soon." And then he's gone. Sharia stares at the spot for a few more seconds before she gets up to wash up and get dressed. As she gets ready for the day, she contemplates the dangers of those men, the Keepers, and if Ji will truly be OK or if he's just bluffing. She also starts thinking about her feelings for him. Were they still just friends? Best friends? More? Her thoughts are interrupted by the television in the room, broadcasting the news.

"Breaking news! Hawaii has gone missing! All of it. The islands, the cities, the people. The entire state is gone. Is this the work of Merc? Experts theorize that it must be. He's the only one who could—" CLICK. She cuts the newscaster off by shutting off the television and then exhales. 'Looks like it's time to go find him again.' She thinks as she smiles at the thought. 'Just like old times. No matter how weird and secretive and dangerous this gets, the situation between us will remain the same.'

She doesn't know how wrong she is.

CHAPTER SEVEN

Sharia and Ji stand together in a random alley, Sharia looking annoyed and Ji looking like his usual self, grinning like an idiot. Sharia has her Keeper robes on and Ji has on a black undershirt tank top with dark blue shorts and black sneakers on his feet. He is also wrapped up in the strange black chains with a white glow that only belong to Keepers, chains that allow no movement and keep him constricted. Despite the uncomfortability of the restraints, Ji still smiles, awaiting his capture. It doesn't take long for the Keepers to come once Sharia calls them in (albeit hesitantly), using the new tech on the back of her hand, and soon enough they show up, secure the prisoner (Ji), and take both Ji and Sharia in a sleek looking black vehicle that almost seems to blend in with the environment.

To say that the car ride is short would be an understatement, lasting only a few seconds, thirty at most, but still Sharia holds Ji's hand as they're moved, patting his hand to keep him calm. In reality the action was done to keep herself calm as Ji is always calm or 'chill' as he says, no matter the situation. This irked her to no end in situations like this. Why can't everyone be rationally afraid like normal people? Her thoughts are interrupted by their arrival at some secret, secure location. Sharia remains silent as they roughly take Ji out of the car, through the doors, and into the building that looks like the lab of an evil scientist. She's not sure what to think and is still worried about Ji and what these men will do to him. One of the three other Keepers with her seems to sense her thoughts and offers an attempt at some reassuring words.

"Don't worry Sharia, we're just taking him into his holding cell. Nothing sinister is going down." He says in his distorted voice. She nods, not really paying much heed to his words. Evil people always insisted that they weren't as evil as they seemed or that their intentions were for the good of everyone. It didn't make them less evil. She walks with the Keepers, stealing glances at Ji to make sure he's OK, but he's still grinning like he's going on a trip to Disneyland or something. She shakes her head at the stupidity of his demeanor, yet at the same time admires his ability to remain composed in the face of danger and what is likely sudden doom.

They continue through the facility, one that seems much larger on the inside than it does on the outside, and Sharia is in wonder at all the strange sights she witnesses. From strange machines to other sleek, future-looking vehicles, to strange sci-fi looking weapons and technology, the entire place seems overwhelming.

"Where are we?" She asks, speaking her first words since she caught Ji, in a distorted voice that surprises her when it leaves her mouth. The Keeper leading Ji throughout the facility answers her without slowing down.

"We are in the Keeper's Crypt, Sharia, where we hold those who are too powerful or...evasive to hold in our normal prisons." He looks towards Ji and continues. "Merc here qualifies for such protocol wouldn't you say?" Sharia nods in agreement with that statement. From what she could see and tell, Ji might even be overqualified to be here. The way he just appeared and disappeared at will, how he easily escaped the Keeper's chains (which she learned earlier were supposed to stop those with powers of any kind from using them), how he was easily able to steal...cities and such? It all still didn't make sense to her, but if you take it all at face value, then Ji is definitely dangerous to the naked eye and definitely belongs here.

Finally they reach a room that's larger than the others and throw Ji in as they begin the lockdown procedure. First, they remove the chains momentarily, just long enough to fit Ji with a straitjacket underneath and then place them back on. In addition to that, they tie the chains to what looks to be a generator of some kind. Not done yet, the Keepers move like clockwork and flip a few switches which generates a force field of energy, likely to keep Ji in. Looking at the spectacle in amazement, Sharia can't keep it in.

"Wow! I didn't even know we had this kind of technology." She says aloud in wonderment, internally flinching at her distorted voice, not used to it just yet. The Keeper next to her looks at her for a moment before turning back to what he's doing.

"You don't." He replies, and Sharia's taken aback. 'What does that mean?' She wonders. 'Just how secret IS this organization.' She then turns her attention back to Ji, wondering if he'll be fine. 'He likely will, or at least he thinks he will. The dummy hasn't stopped smiling since we got here. But still…I can't help but worry.' She thinks to herself.

"OK, we're done with the preliminary constraints. Now do your thing, we'll be out here waiting." Instructs the Keeper closest to her. She nods and walks in the room, slowly, taking it all in as she makes her way to Ji.

"Ji, are you…are you OK?" She asks, unable to help herself, going straight to the source to ease her worrying, though she knows deep down that he would never admit if he wasn't.

"I'm good, thanks for asking." He replies nonchalantly with a nod, the only movement he can make since everything from the neck down is restrained. "How are you holding up?" He asks, noticing her constant state of worry since she captured him in her chains. Sharia hesitates, looking at the ground.

"I…I'm not sure." Sharia begins. "This is all so new to me, and so weird. And to see you like that…it almost seems like it isn't right." She clarifies.

"Nonsense." Says Ji without a care in the world. "I steal things, and you hate stealing. So naturally, you want to see me locked up at least on some level." He reasons. Sharia nods slowly. 'it's true' she thinks to herself.

"But not like this." She says almost in a pleading voice. "It just looks so…restricting. I know you can eat but…how will you use the bathroom? Or bathe? Or…or sleep?" She questions, rattling off life essentials that he definitely couldn't do restrained as he was. To his credit, Ji doesn't seem to be fazed by these thoughts or restrictions.

"I probably won't." He replies with a shrug. He then grins, a thought coming to his mind. "Unless you want to help me with those." He speaks in a suggestive tone as he licks his lips. Sharia isn't amused by his antics.

"Be serious, Ji! Now's not the time for jokes!" She yells at him.

"I was." He mutters to himself. Sharia ignores him.

"I think...I think you should go ahead and give these men what they want." She says with a shaky voice that sounds odd with the distortion caused by her new Keeper status, clearly scared for Ji's wellbeing.

"Never." He exclaims with an intense tone. He then softens it as he continues. "I'll only give you what you want." He says, looking her in the eyes, staring deep into her heart and soul. "What do you want, Sharia."

'You.' She thinks for a moment, the word on the tip of her tongue, much to her own surprise. She shakes her head to rid herself of such thoughts. Now was not the time. 'You to be free, not so helpless.' She thinks once she reformulates her thoughts.

"I want..." She stops to take a deep breath, contemplating saying what she was thinking. She decides against it. "Never mind, just return Hawaii. Please?" She begs him. Ji twitches.

"OK, done." He says. Sharia looks back at the other Keepers and nods. They take that as the signal and immediately get on the phone and check the tech on the back of their hands to make sure. The men nod and speak amongst themselves, confirming the results and that Hawaii is in fact back in its correct place. After that, one of the Keepers comes into the room, beckoning her to leave.

"Excellent work Miss Sharia. Now, it's time to finish applying the restraints so we'll need to leave the room." He informs her. She nods in affirmation and takes one last longing look at Ji, almost unwilling to leave him in here to be subject to the whims of these men. Ji gives her a grin and a wink which calms her down some, allowing her to confidently leave the room with knowledge that he would be OK. She then turns and follows the Keeper out of the room as they get back to the controls from before. As soon as they exit the room, the Keeper with her speaks her praises once more.

"Again, great work Agent Ihuwaki." He addresses her more formally this time. She nods once more and looks back at the room where Ji was constricted.

"Thank you." She says in a tone just above a whisper, barely audible with the voice distortion. The Keeper then turns to the other Keeper, the one at the controls and issues a command.

"Put the room in level twelve lockdown." This clearly surprises the other Keeper who turns his head sharply and asks for clarification.

"Level *twelve* sir?" He asks, making sure he heard correctly and that they really wanted to go this far. The Keeper with Sharia doesn't even move his gaze from the room and Ji's person.

"I didn't stutter." He says in a stern voice. The other Keeper nods and gets back to work.

"Yes sir, right away." He complies as he hits several buttons in a row. The question is now nagging in the back of Sharia's mind and she has to know, to know exactly what they were going to subject Ji to.

"What's level twelve?" She asks, turning to the Keeper. Again he doesn't take his eyes off of the room and the prisoner inside.

"It's a special kind of lockdown that no *one* or *thing* can escape from." He begins. "Special energy fields, powerful and unbreakable walls, force fields on top of force fields, electrical locks on the nerves in the body, laser fields, the whole works." He describes, clearly proud of the level twelve lockdown and all the features it contain. "You'd have to bend time and space to escape." He adds on, finishing his statement. This only makes Sharia worry even more.

"Will he be alright?" She questions aloud. Again, the Keeper doesn't look at her when he answers.

"He'll be fine Miss Sharia— no, Agent Iwuhaki. Don't worry so much." She nods in understanding, but thinks otherwise to herself. 'I don't believe him in the way he means it, but I know Ji will be fine.' She thinks. 'I just do.'

"Level twelve lockdown complete sir. He won't be getting out of there." Confirms the Keeper at the controls. The Keeper next to Sharia smiles in relief.

"Good. We've finally—" Before he can say much, the alarm rings, a loud siren flowing throughout the building with as a red light shines over the place. As the siren wails, a robotic voice speaks over it.

"Breach in level twelve containment! Breach in level twelve containment!" States the voice over and over again on constant repeat. Sharia is startled by the initial alarm but calms herself down. The other Keepers don't have as much luck.

"What? What's happening!" Asks the Keeper nearest to her, yelling loudly at the Keeper at the controls.

"I...I don't know sir. It seems like he's broken through level twelve lockdown." Explains the Keeper.

"Impossible!" Exclaims the Keeper closest to her. "No one has ever—!"

"Well he did sir. I don't know how, but he did." Explains the Keeper at the controls.

"Sonics failed to stop target! Use of teleporters permitted!" Comes the robotic voice accompanying the alarm. "Teleporters failed!"

"What's happening?" Asks Sharia looking around, though she has an idea based on the words stringing out from the alarm system.

"He escaped." Says the Keeper closest to her, breathing it out in disbelief. "He really escaped."

She nods meekly at the declaration, but then looks away with a small smile. 'I knew you'd be fine.' She thinks, relieved at the turn of events.

CHAPTER EIGHT

"Breaking news! All of China, gone!" That is the headline on every channel in the country right now, detailing what is likely Ji's latest escapade, making China disappear, or as he'd call it 'stealing China.' But unlike his other escapades, his other triumphs, this one was on its way to causing something much worse. Something akin to World War III. See, the other conquests, the other victims of Ji's stealing were either allies of the United States, too small to be a real threat to the United States, or in awe of their national treasure being taken so suddenly. This was not the case with the likes of China, or at least it's assumed that it wouldn't be the case, whenever they were returned and were actually able to retaliate. There was a chance that they wouldn't, but now with all the gas lighting from American television and eyes on them from all around the world, their hand will be forced. And then there's the Russia factor.

Somehow, some way, Russia managed to insert themselves into this situation, despite not being affected at all. Their leaders took to the press and claimed that America needed to be stopped and that if they could do it to China, a rival super power, they could and would do it to anyone. Of course they don't take into account the fact that Ji's working on his own and *not* in the interests of the United States, AND that Ji is currently a criminal of said country. Also, at the moment Ji is literally being hunted down for the exact crime of taking China despite such the crime not technically landing within United States jurisdiction. America is actually doing everything it can to try to help the situation, more than it should logically, and still they're getting blamed. We're getting blamed.

Sharia cuts off her thoughts as she looks back at the television where a pretty heated debate is going on at the moment, about the very same topic her thoughts wandered to.

"The question is," begins one of the debaters, an older brown-skinned male with a bushy mustache and balding head "who did this? Once we find that out, we can figure out his nationality and exactly who should be held responsible for the crime." He explains. The other debater, a younger woman with pale skin and dark brown hair rebuttals immediately.

"There is *no* question of who did this, Jerry. It's obviously 'Merc' AKA 'Mercury' the thief that was responsible for the Seven Wonders Heist, and the only one even capable of doing this. And with that *obvious* piece of knowledge, what we really have to question is...how responsible *is* the United States for what's happened? This Merc is an American citizen after all and his actions reflect on the country whether they like it or not." She counters. The first debater, Jerry, responds immediately.

"OK, Anne. Let's assume that this is 'Merc', not that we have any proof, but let's assume it is him. How does the United States take any responsibility for his actions? Merc is a wanted criminal in the United States and has been for nearly half a decade. It's clear the country doesn't condone and certainly doesn't endorse his actions, so why? Why would they take the blame for one criminal's misdeeds; one that they're trying to catch and are actively working against at that?" This statement causes Anne to roll her eyes as she responds in an incredulous tone.

"Are you serious Jerry? Has the United States *never* used a criminal to its own advantage? Do those countless South American dictators ring a bell? And are you telling me that out of all the countries in the world, that this Merc just happened to pick China? America's biggest rivals? You can't tell me that's a coincidence. It's clear that the United States is doing a test run with this Merc, working with him in a plan to take down their competition. Anyone who denies it is full of it!" Jerry rubs his temples and closes his eyes before responding in a calmer tone.

"Or, maybe Merc simply wanted a country that would cause a lot of ruckus, is well known, AND has an obscene amount of people living within its borders. China fits the bill on all of these Anne. To automatically point to this Merc being a weapon, and to say without a doubt that he's working with the United States is disingenuous at best." Sharia now rolls her eyes, not willing to listen to the news debate things they couldn't possibly know for another second, and turns off the television.

"Damn Ji, this time you really did go too far." She says out loud. "This could start a war and affect us all." Suddenly her television seems to turn itself on somehow, causing her to eye the remote with a weary eye. Hesitantly she looks up at the television and sees something she thought she'd never see in…well ever. It's Ji on the screen, addressing the people, somehow making himself appear on an extra split screen alongside the other debaters and newscasters. He's wearing a black trench coat, a black button up shirt, black pants, and black construction boots and appears to be on some stage, in front of a microphone and in front of a large crowd. Wait, from the looks of it that's…no he wouldn't. Would he?

"Hello world, this is Merc, the world's greatest thief speaking to you from China. Yes, I said China. First and foremost, I want to announce that I've returned China now and you can all stop your whining and complaining and blaming of whoever. I act on my own and to try to attribute my actions to anyone else, is insulting to me. Because of your foolishness, and readiness to start a war over literally nothing, I've taken your weapons. All of them. Guns, bullets, missiles, tanks, nukes, you name it. Call it the Mass Disarmament Heist." He says, pausing for a moment. "Now I got work to do. With a country under my belt, a continent is calling my name." He informs them as he drops the mic and disappears without a trace. Immediately everyone starts talking, yelling even on what just transpired and what continent he would steal.

"Will it be Asia?" Starts one man, a middle-aged fat male with tan skin and white hair. "I think it will be. Merc will finish what he started and take the largest continent on the Earth, population-wise."

"No it can't be Asia." Rebuts Anne from the last argument. "It'd be redundant and we all know that Merc doesn't do redundancy. It'd encompass *both* of his former heists and that would be too plain for him." She explains.

"Then North America?" Counters the same man. She waves this answer off as well.

"No, of course not. It's where Merc lives. One doesn't steal their own home." She reasons. "I for one, think it'll be Europe. It's small, so I assume it'll be easier to steal, yet impactful enough that the results will be felt around the world."

"Of course, that makes so much sense. It's definitely Europe after hearing that." Says the middle-aged fat man in agreement.

"I'd have to agree with Anne on that. Europe is too good to pass up and has many iconic countries within its borders." Says another man, this one younger looking with a sleek face, slick black hair, and thin glasses.

"What about Australia?" Asks an old yet thin Hispanic man, another of the debaters.

"Too poisonous. No one would want to mess with that continent." Says Anne, dismissing the choice with a haughty laugh.

"But wouldn't the danger be part of the thrill? Part of the fun for him?" Argues the Hispanic man.

"Maybe, but it doesn't seem like his style." Interjects the middle-aged fat man.

"What about Africa? It is the richest continent by far, especially if we consider its natural resources." Points out a young black woman with straight black hair. Anne and the Hispanic man nod in agreement.

"That is true." Says Anne.

"A good point." Concedes the middle-aged fat man.

"That's my personal choice." Chimes in Jerry from before. Again, not willing to listen to them continue to argue about nothing, Sharia shuts off the television, hoping it stays off this time.

Truthfully Sharia is utterly shocked and still in awe that Ji would ever do such a thing. It wasn't just him interrupting news casts, and appearing on national and possibly global television, but it was also him giving up his heist AND announcing his next one. Or at least parts of his next one. And stealing the weapons? It seems that Ji understood exactly what his heist did and made sure to do everything in his power to fix it. And that made her very proud of him and his maturity and how much he's grown. As she always said, there's a good person underneath he thief that is Ohiji Olezuo. And it's not that hard to find if one just looks. The situation brightened her mood for the entire rest of the day. It made her feel so positive, that she didn't even mind when Antarctica went missing an hour later when Ji made his decision on which continent to steal.

Much like China before it, Antarctica drops completely off of every map in the world, any search engine, and any navigation system. It appears that when Ji steals something, he really does take it from any and every one. With a sigh, Sharia gets dressed in her keeper robes and wears her hair in braided plaits and starts on her journey to find Ji and bring him in, just like old times she supposed. But it wasn't like old times, and she knew it. She saw what the Keepers, her new organization, tried to do to him. Normal prison could never replicate that or begin to even try. He might've broken free and escaped, but it didn't change the fact that the stakes are much higher now as he's dealing with people who are far more dangerous than he's used to. And for some reason, she was helping them and not him.

That bugged her to no end and she couldn't really find a good answer as to why. Sure, she wants Ji to be brought to justice and to stop his thievery, but not at the cost of his facilities like the Keepers seem to want. Ji is her friend and she knows that deep down she should be helping him instead of hindering, but her hate for stealing won't allow it. So here they are, best friends on the opposite side of the law; thief who constantly escapes and the officer, now Keeper, who brings him in. It was a strange relationship to say the least. Shaking the thoughts from her head, she focuses on finding Ji.

With her knowledge of Ji and her new Keeper status, it doesn't take her long to find him. He seems to be expecting her as he turns and waves to her as she walks onto the scene. And of course, he's still grinning like an idiot. As Sharia reaches him, she instantly blurts out the question that's been on her mind since she heard about the China heist.

"Why?" Is all she says, though it says enough. Why did he steal China? Why did he steal Antarctica? Why did he steal at all and keep escalating the objects he stole until they reached insane heights as they had now?

"To test myself." He answers. "As the world's greatest thief, it's hard to inherently know my limits. So I got to keep trying more and more, climbing higher and higher until I finally find something I can't steal." He explains. "Though I'm not sure something like that exists." He adds with clear subtext. If it does, he *will* find out, even if he has to keep escalating his heists into unseen territories. Sharia nods in understanding, as testing one's limits is a common motive. It just usually is tested in things like weight lifting, or running fast, or video games, and a limit tends to be reached. She's not sure Ji will ever reach a limit and he might just keep stealing forever and ever, for all of eternity, continuing their friendly game of cop and robber.

"When are your friends coming?" He asks, breaking her out of her thoughts, referring to the Keepers.

"I...I don't know." She responds truthfully. Her job is to find him, restrain him, and bring him in. She's never received any word on exactly how long it takes Keepers to respond to her signal, though they do seem to appear pretty quickly.

"Want to chill while we wait for them?" He asks sincerely.

"Sure." She says with a smile as she walks next to him and sits down. He does the same and both of them sit in relative silence, enjoying each other's company for a solid minute until the Keepers show up, twenty deep. With a sigh, Sharia knows they have to end their 'chill' time as she stands up and pulls out her chains. Ji stands up with her and patiently waits for her to chain him up as she did before, and lead him to the Keepers. This time she doesn't go with him, declining her colleagues' offer to ride with her thieving friend, and watches him leave with a strange feeling in her stomach. For some reason, she feels like this will be the last they see of each other in a long time and internally she's choking up a bit. Her rational side tells her to go with him, spend as much time as she can before whatever happens, happens, but she can't bring herself to do it, as it'd just make it that much harder. Instead she gives him a small smile and waves goodbye until the Keeper vehicle disappears from her sight, on its way to the Keeper's Crypt no doubt.

With a deep breath, Sharia turns tail and heads back home, feeling empty and spineless for not following her rational side and taking the trip with ji. What if he needed her? What if the Keepers were too rough on him and he got hurt? What if...? She stops the train of thought before she goes crazy with worry. It doesn't do good to come up with hypothetical bad situations and she knows it. Instead she occupies her mind with wondering what it is exactly that will cause this to be the last time she sees Ji in a long time.

Death. Imprisonment. Exile. All three ideas permeate her thoughts immediately before she can stop herself. Her breath becomes shaky as she tries to move past those into more positive things. Like...maybe Ji will simply be too busy making an honest living so she won't interact with him much anymore (Due to her being a Keeper now)? Or maybe she'll get real into her Keeper job and move up the ranks, thus having less time to see him? Or maybe...maybe she's just being silly about the feeling and nothing was going to happen? That one is easily her favorite of the situations, but one she doubts is true.

As she finally reaches home and removes her Keeper robe and technology, she notices a note on her door from Ji. It looks like Ji has already escaped from the Keepers (he did so in less than five minutes) and has thus left her something for her troubles. She smiles at the thought and picks up the note, reading it over.

Dear Sharia,

I escaped from your friends as I got bored without you there to hold things down. I would've escaped even if you were there, but I'd at least wait until we had some 'fun' in interrogation. That's always the best part. Anyways, I'm going away for a while to explore new heights in my thievery as I've done everything I can here, what with stealing an entire continent. Oh, and speaking of continents, I did you a solid and returned Antarctica for you, not that anyone was missing it, so you can claim that on your Keeper resume or record or whatever it is you keep. Hope your Keeper job continues going well without me there, and I'll miss you. A lot.

P.S. I also stole all things money (or is it monetary?) in the world as I left. I figured I might as well complete the one-two punch, along with the weapons I stole earlier, to make the world a better place.

Ash she gets to the end of the letter, Sharia smiles once more, happy again at Ji's growth that he's actually thinking of the betterment of the world. She does wonder exactly how no money and no guns will change things, but quickly wipes that from her mind. More important things have happened, are happening. For the first time in a long time, she wouldn't be able to see her dearest friend Ji and would have to live life completely without him. It looks like her feeling came true and...it didn't feel good. She'd rather have been wrong than to feel how she felt right now if she was honest with herself. Like he said, she'd miss him. A lot. And she'd await his return.

CHAPTER NINE

Ji has finally done it. He has finally transcended Earth itself in his thievery and is going where no man has gone before: outer space. And by going to outer space, he means *real* outer space. Not just the Moon or Mars like Neil Armstrong and little NASA drones, but other solar systems and galaxies with life to experience, cultures to learn, people to meet, and more importantly things to steal. There is a catch however, as the majority of the planets he will visit can't be survived by humans, as in their atmosphere is toxic in some way to the human body. Sometimes it's extreme cold, sometimes it's poisonous gas, sometimes it's extreme heat, and sometimes it's simply a lack of oxygen in the air. Either way, without his special brand of thievery, he couldn't be getting very far.

The planet he's on now is very much like Earth in its atmosphere; it simply lacks oxygen and nitrogen and instead has primarily helium and hydrogen in its air. Besides that, it's very similar. The people look the same, even mirroring the races and features of humans, the clothing is similar albeit a bit more fantasy-esque with more robes, scarfs, and sashes, and the food is close to the same though with a hint of...something that makes everything taste slightly off. This is likely due to the food being made with similar plants and animals as Earth, but with the chemistry change adding to it. Ji didn't mind the differences and in fact relishes them as he explores the unknown. He knows not every planet is like this one due to the previous planet he was just one.

That planet was basically a super hot, volcanic planet, with magma coursing through the crust of the planet and the core of the planet being basically a ball of super-heated plasma around ionized gas. The temperature on that planet was insane as one can imagine. It was so hot that Ji immediately caught fire just by stepping foot on the planet. It took some quick thinking and super thievery to quell the flames and allow his body to get used to it, but if Ji knew anything about humans, or even Earth, he'd confidently say that a normal human would be vaporized by the heat and that any kind of Earthly metal would be turned to liquid, immediately melting on contact. It was crazy hot, next-level heat and nothing could survive there that wasn't ready for it or born for the heat. Beyond the heat, the planet was covered entirely in volcanic rock, or lavarock as he called it. There were entire continents of Obsidian, and…other lavarocks he didn't know the name of, that had countries of different sub-class of lavarocks in them. The seas and oceans of Earth were now seas and oceans of super-hot lava, and on this planet there was no day and night, just one time of day with moderate amounts of star light. Where Earth had hills and mountains, lakes, and rivers and such, this planet was all volcanos and geysers, lakes and rivers of lava. The best thing about the planet was the inhabitants.

On the planet there were still 'people' and 'animals' per say, but they weren't exactly the same. The 'people' were…humanoid enough, with skin that was more like armor, to protect them from and conduct the heat, and blood more like molten metal when it came out. They were super dark in color due to the extreme heat and had glowing lava colored eyes, but no hair. The males were obvious as they were taller and bulkier by a good three feet in height and foot in width, as females were as thin as normal human males, but with curvier more voluptuous shapes. The 'people' also seemed to vary in shininess of their armor-like skin, and their heights and widths rather than color. The 'animals' of the planets were basically walking lava constructs, shaped like various things. There were deer-like constructs, and bear-like constructs, but differences made them more…alien (duh). Like a random lavabeast (as he called them) could have eight legs or two heads or five tails at any time. They difference in sizes seemed to be how they categorized and differentiated themselves, though most of the lavabeasts ran alone rather than in packs. Another big difference is that the 'people' and 'animals' had very little interaction. The 'people' literally consumed the everlasting lava supply from the bowels of the planet, while the 'animals' mostly bathed in it, absorbing more lava for their being to grow. Somehow this didn't result in the 'people' hunting the 'animals' or lavabeast as for some reason, 'animals' or lavabeasts weren't in a correct form that the 'people' could properly process their lava for food. It was just easier to stop by the many lakes or rivers or the giant oceans to feast, rather than to try to figure out a way to change the lavabeasts into edible food. Ultimately there wasn't much to steal from that planet, besides a few cool lavabeast pets, so now Ji is here on this Earth-like planet, planning a heist.

A heist of what? One may ask. Well it's simple…Ji doesn't know yet. See Ji's main goal at the time is to explore these other planets, taking his time to do so, and in the process find out their treasures. He wants something priceless from each one, sort of like a trophy for his outer-planet thievery. At first he contemplated 'taking' women from each planet, but nah, there's only one woman for him. Plus he didn't want space AIDS (a joke, he'd just steal it from himself).

And so Ji spent the necessary time to fully explore the planet, posing as one of its natives, and going through everyday life looking for something special to steal (outside of money). Ultimately, he scouts out a potential target on a trip to a museum. Apparently they held some ancient relic in the museum that was supposed to be 'one of a kind.' He only caught a glimpse of it as he glossed over what the tour guide was saying, but it was clearly behind a lot of security and on constant watch. This caused Ji to wear one of his trademark grins, as that is his kind of heist.

While Ji could actually try and easily steal the relic in an instant, there was no fun in that here. He knew these priceless artifacts weren't beyond his limits, so there was no need to go so hard. Plus She wasn't even here to show off to, so it was useless. Instead Ji goes through the old steps, just like he did when he was younger. First, he stakes out the place, watching the museum, taking notes on shifts and types of security and times when it's best to infiltrate and begin thieving. He then picks the perfect night to sneak in, easily infiltrating the museum as he comes upon the relic, behind tons of laser security and alarms. Apparently, this relic is a super-condensed star of some kind, a mini-frozen supernova to be exact. 'Awesome' is the only word he thinks as he reaches out and snatches the relic without tripping any alarm, easily bypassing the security.

Ji shakes his head and acts sheepishly as he realizes that he moved entirely on muscle memory and used some of his advanced skills despite holding back on the theft. With a sigh, Ji purposely trips several alarms on the way out to make up for it, also to make sure someone would try to follow him and apprehend him (maybe he missed Her a little too much). He also can't wait to be introduced to the space police and see what kind of cool stuff they have. With those thoughts in mind, Ji escapes the museum and heads to the space port. There he manages to hitch a ride (without the knowledge of the driver of course) off-world on a random space ship version of an SUV (big and homely, less cool looking, less sleek).

Ji remains on the ship for a while until he notices that the driver and likely owner of the ship is planning a long-range flight and a far longer trip than Ji felt like taking. So with expert precision and grace that only Earth's Greatest Thief could possess, Ji ejects himself from the ship and freefalls onto the next planet. On the way down, he's forced to steal a lot of things from himself, the need to breathe, the need for any kind of heat (amongst other things to survive the vacuum of space), momentum in any direction but the one he needed, and the ability to feel pain and take any kind of damage. Otherwise Ji would just be a dead human floating in space or a burnt husk in the atmosphere or a bloody smear on the ground, depending on when he slacked off. Either way it all happens in about a second, not giving the space police much time to react.

As Ji gets to his feet, he takes the time to look around the planet and see where he is, or at least what kind of planet he's on. His initial impression is...gaseous. Yellow gas is all he sees, touches, hears, smells, and breathes for seemingly miles upon miles around his location. The air has a gaseous haze, the ground has a gaseous haze, the star is blocked by gaseous haze, everything is gaseous haze. The haze is thick too, not allowing much for visibility (if he wasn't the greatest thief), which makes it hard to tell if there's much of a ground underneath. And even worse, the gas is poisonous to normal humans. Maybe with a bit more exploring, he could find something, but right now this place isn't looking too promising.

'I wonder how Ji is doing.' Thinks Sharia as she becomes bored with television, especially the constant debates on the news about if the world will fall or be a better place thanks to Merc (and his thievery of all weapons and money). The debaters constantly bringing up Merc didn't help in Sharia's task to forget about Ji for now and focus on life, and it helped even less when she's called in by the Keepers and the message says it's specifically about Ji or 'Merc' as they call him, much like everyone else. 'Why do they call him that?' She wonders to herself. It's clear they know of his real name and have used it before when identifying him, but for the most part they stick to 'Merc' like the rest of the public. Did...did Ji possibly do his weird thief thing and steal something impossible from them? Like the knowledge of his identity? Or did they simply choose not to use it? She couldn't decide which made more sense and was the better answer. Regardless, she was just called in, so it was time to get ready.

Ji uses his abilities to explore the planet as fast as possible and finds nothing of worth. Just all gas as he initially thought. The planet isn't barren of life or anything, it has people, animals, plants, civilizations, buildings, governments, weather, clouds, etc. It has everything. The problem is that everything is just gas. All of it is made of the yellow gas, albeit with different tints in some places. If he was a scientist, Ji would admit that it was fascinating to witness, a sight to behold: humanized gas with thoughts, personalities, feelings, etc. as well as some form of semi-solid gas that could hold together in shapes and such. It just...defies all common sense and logic, especially the weather where there are clouds of gas (what else is new?) but also rain made of semi-liquid gas, as well as snow, sleet, hail, etc. They have food made of gas, furniture made of gas, money made of gas, the whole works. They have so-called priceless artifacts in buildings, but all of them are made of gas. Ji CAN steal the gas in any form or shape and keep it that way, trademarks of a great thief, but it just didn't strike him as...worth it really. The whole thing is a bust as far as he's concerned. Time to get a ride out of here. 'I wonder, should I steal the knowledge of which planets to explore?' He thinks to himself. 'Nah. That's half of the fun!' He decides internally.

Sharia, finished with washing up, eating, and generally prepping herself for contact with the outside world, dons her Keeper's robe and her Keeper technology as she leaves the house to her 'special' meeting they called her for. Only moments after she leaves the house, does Sharia get somewhat worried. 'What did they call me for?' She wonders. 'I hope it's nothing bad…' Her thoughts trail off. 'Wait, did something happen to Ji maybe? Are they delivering the bad news?' She asks herself. She then shakes her head. 'No, they wouldn't call a special meeting just for that. They'd just wait until we next saw each other.' She decides internally. 'So what is it then? Have they maybe located Ji and need me to capture him again?' She thinks hopefully. She knows that she longs to see him again, and being called to catch Ji would be much like old times. Sharia also knows that it's not likely and that he was gone for a while of his own admission. It's very unlikely he'll return any time soon. When Ji went exploring, when he went looking for something, he went all in. That's just the way he was. She smiles at her reminiscent thoughts of Ji as she makes it to the facility, this one looking more like the base for an evil NASA, using her Keeper-issued vehicle to make the trip short. With a deep breath, she steps inside and stares in wonder at the futuristic looking building with a beautiful design to it. The walls are shiny and the windows sparkle. The floor is shiny as well and the ceiling appears endless and infinite as it's out of her vision. Each room on the initial floor looks more like a portal than a room, and no doubt each leads to a different place entirely, rather than just a section of the building like a normal room.

Quickly she walks past the various rooms to the transporter, the Keeper version of an elevator that takes the person through some kind of portal to the destination they need to reach. In this case, the transporter is keyed only to the floors in this building and the rooms on these floors. She quickly hits the sixth floor, and appears there instantly, a bit shaken by the jostling around of her insides. According to the other Keepers, and her Keeper's manual, this was normal for new Keepers to experience. In time she would get tougher and more used to the feeling. She then walks into the room and sees the two Keepers who recruited her, waiting for her arrival.

"Ah, Agent Iwuhaki." Acknowledges one of the Keepers as the other simply nods in her direction. The Keeper that speaks even gets up hurriedly and offers a handshake, something that Sharia takes him up on. "A pleasure to see you again." He exclaims in his distorted voice as their hands detach. "Please, take a seat." He all but commands. Sharia nods and takes a seat, speaking as she does.

"Pleasure to see you two...too." She says awkwardly with a smile.

"Of course." Says the second Keeper, the one who stayed seated. "Now let's not waste time and get right to the reason why we called you here today."

"Agent Iwuhaki." Begins the first Keeper, the one who greeted her. "Do you know where Merc is right now?"

"Or where he went?" Chimes in the other Keeper. Sharia looks surprised that they seem to know that he's gone already. After she recovers, she does the only thing she can do in this situation: answer truthfully.

"I don't, I'm sorry." She replies. This seems to throw the Keepers through a loop.

"I see..." Says the second Keeper.

"How unexpected." Says the first Keeper, both of them obviously deep in thought.

"Do you think he's left the planet?" Asks the second Keeper, directing his question to the first Keeper.

"It's a possibility, but not one we should see as concrete just yet. Our sensors are unreliable when it comes to Merc, and honestly Agent Iwuhaki is our most valuable resource when it concerns him. What do you think Sharia?" He ends his statement, inquiring her. Sharia is taken aback by the casual conversation they just had in front of her about *travelling to other planets*. Like...what? This was blowing her mind and she could barely even grasp the concept, even after all that she's seen from Ji. 'Can he even do that?' She wonders internally. She then realizes that they're waiting on her response and parrots her thoughts.

"...Can he even do that?" She asks in a confused tone. It told the Keepers all they needed to know. Sharia wouldn't know if Merc was off-world. She really didn't have the information they required.

Ji is now on another world, this one a stark contrast to the volcanic planet from before. This planet is super, super cold, and seems more like the planet he left with the museum in that the people are very human-like, though they're pale white with glowing blue eyes this time. Back to the cold though. This planet is so cold that if he wasn't who he is, every drop of liquid inside of his body would freeze upon entry. It's so cold that it could freeze fire—no lava in an instant. He's almost convinced it can freeze the sun, but he knows better due to science and all that jazz. Speaking of suns, it seemed that this planet lacked one as in addition to the super cold, there is no light on this planet, it's covered in complete darkness. Again if he wasn't who he is, he wouldn't be able to see even a centimeter out in front of him. From that alone he concludes that the people, the natives on this planet have some form of night vision.

As he explores the planet, he notices that much of it is like Earth and the planet he just left. It seems that buildings, civilizations, transportation, etc. is a common thing on planets with life. Though also like that other planet, he notices that it's more technologically advanced, being privy to space travel and other technology that belonged in a sci-fi or future-world type show or cartoon. From hovering and flying vehicles to using things like nanites and other medical advances so seamlessly, as well as the abundance of lasers, it's easy to tell that the planet is beyond Earth at the time. As he's on the planet he also notices a huge issue, not unlike any other world he's bound to be on he assumes, that the natives speak alien tongue (or their own tongue since *he*'s the alien to them) and he couldn't understand a word of it. Somehow the last planet (not counting the gaseous planet) seemed to have something where he could inherently understand the people and the words they said and wrote. Was it advanced translator technology, or his brain and stealing ability working subconsciously for him to counter his stupidity? He honestly couldn't tell at the moment. Either way he's forced to steal basic knowledge from random people's heads so he can speak and read the language.

Once that's acquired, Ji uses his abilities to blend in and wander the area, the planet as he did all others. Besides trying exquisite frozen cuisine and going sight-seeing, Ji does manage to locate exactly what he'll steal next: the treasure of their planet, a small sliver of the star that used to warm the cold, dark planet before it went out and presumably nova or something (he's iffy on the details). He wonders briefly if all the relics will be pieces of stars or of that nature. 'Maybe I should just skip right to stealing those then..." He thinks, his thoughts trailing off. 'Nah.' He shakes off the feeling. It was best to work his way up to stealing actual and literal stars. One didn't want to run before walking after all. Not even a thief who can steal everything.

Again, like the museum on the other planet, Ji takes the steps to do this the old-fashioned way, staking out the sacred temple where they held their treasure and checking for any traps and/or security. Nothing there is too concerning for him, so he plans the heist for later that day. He takes the time to admire some of the natives of the planet, and notices that the women are very beautiful in their own way. They aren't his type exactly, but still they're nice on the eyes and a good distraction until it's go time. When it is finally go time, Ji almost doesn't want to go, clearly enjoying the view more than he should. Reluctantly and with a sigh he leaves his spot and makes his way to the temple. With super agility he weaves his way through traps, avoiding any guards and surveillance technology as he does and easily reaches the treasure he came here for. With the traps sprung, he calmly walks out of the temple and makes sure to take his time setting off every alarm he can as he does. He takes a final look at the planet, admiring the view one last time before leaving. 'Oh well, time to take off.' He thinks to himself. 'I wonder...I set off all of those alarms and I don't—' his thoughts are interrupted by several white shiny, sleek space ships descending upon his location. 'Yes! Space police! Awesome.' He thinks with a grin.

"Stop where you are and hand over the treasures. If you don't we will be forced to apprehend you to the best of our ability and to the fullest extent of the law!" Comes the PA-like announcement from the space police cars. Just like the former planet, the space police seem to have translator technology so that everyone can understand them. 'Make sense given what they do.' Thinks Ji with a shrug. He then thinks on the best way to respond to the space police.

Should he go flashy and put on a show for them? Or should he simply escape without saying a word? Or maybe he should stick around and antagonize them with taunts and such?

"Nah." He says, shaking his head both at his own thoughts and at the space police. Immediately he's forced to run as he dodges shots from their laser guns on instinct. 'I see they're all kill and no talk here.' He thinks as he dodges his twentieth laser beam. 'Time to bounce for real.' He thinks as he steals the ammo for all of their guns, and even steals a gun from one of them for...future use. 'Why stop there?' He wonders to himself. He goes the full mile and steals one of their ships to take off world to his next stop, the irony not lost on him as he thinks his final on-world thoughts.

'This is the life.'

CHAPTER TEN

'I wonder if he'll ever come back'. Thinks Sharia to herself, thinking back to Ji despite her desire to try and forget him. If she's honest with herself, she misses him dearly. 'He's been gone for three months already. How much longer will it be?' She wonders. 'At least he returned Antarctica before she left.' She admits, relieved. It'd be a nightmare if he hadn't. The whole debacle with China proved that. Somehow the entire country would be blamed for Ji's actions, though it wouldn't be quite as bad this time as Antarctica isn't exactly inhabited, nor is it one of the few superpowers in the world. Still, it would be a headache so she's thankful he didn't leave things up in the air.

She then thinks to the current changes the world is going through. With no weapons, the dynamics of war have changed greatly. Now China is top dog due to an overwhelming population, and in an attempt to counter such advantages, martial arts and close combat training have become popular. Somehow all attempts to make any kind of weapon seem to just...fail. Complex weapons and the blueprints and knowhow on making them has disappeared, but even medieval weapons like a spear, sword, bow and arrow, and such just can't be made. The most that seems to be allowed is a bat or a stick or something in normal everyday life such as a mop, that can be commandeered as a weapon. And even then, no sharpening it or enhancing it. It just didn't work. Ji has really changed life on Earth as people know it.

Even more, with the lack of money and all things monetary, a lot has changed with inventions and technology period. Once people stopped holding out in hopes of money somehow reappearing, the level of technology on Earth rose tenfold in just a month. Technology hoarded by companies hoping to make a good buck (read: billions of dollars) has now been released, and with no weapons being possible, even governments have released their technology to the world. Life in general is much better with everything being free, and people getting everything they need without any real cost. She's sure that soon Earth will be a utopia, and it will all be thanks to Ji. The very thought of it brings a wide smile to Sharia's face.

It looks like she was right about him being a good person, but ultimately wrong about hating his stealing as it's brought more good to the planet than anything else ever has or ever could. If Ji weren't such a close friend, she might even owe him an apology. Whenever he got back that is.

But for now, life was good, or as good as it could be without him. She's still with the Keepers despite his absence, and with them she's learned a lot of things. Useful things. Like how to operate high level technology, how to make high level technology, how to track and find nearly anyone or anything on the planet, etc. Interestingly enough the Keepers seem to be the one thing, the one group or organization unaffected by the stealing. For whatever reason, Ji seems to have spared them. Sharia couldn't help to think that it's because of her that he did so. He did claim he doesn't steal from her so maybe he saw them as an extension of her by proxy. She also couldn't help the feeling that maybe he simply enjoyed the chase and the...presence of an enemy, of a police force that the Keepers provided, and that's why he let them keep their weapons (word play noted). Without them, they'd be no more than common police man or high tech agents that are useless in a fight. Either way, life was interesting for her as she tried to move on without the excitement he brought into her life, and instead replace it with the excitement of being a Keeper.

Ji whistles as he lays back in a brand new space ship that he stole from the King of some slime planet he was just on. The planet was pretty cool but also very monotonous. There was green slime everywhere, and it was very...vibrant. Everything on the planet was either made of slime or leaked slime like it was condensation. There was everything from geysers, rivers, volcanos, etc. of slime to even the grass itself leaking slime. The people were just stereotypical globs of slime, but they were somewhat sophisticated in their culture and technology. Overall, Ji was able to blend in, walk on top of all the slime, and steal both a ship to escape on and their prime slime ball. Ji holds up the ball as he thinks about it, looking it over once more. The ball is about the size of his palm and it's made of glowing black slime. It's not lost on him that this is no different than the main treasure on the gaseous planet he left earlier and had declared useless, so he vowed to make sure to go steal that super-gas-treasure-thing as soon as he wasn't busy moving forward with these other planets. If he tried, it wouldn't take more than an instant, so it's not like it'd be a time-wasting endeavor. He then turns back to the treasured slime ball in his hand. 'I wonder if it's radioactive.' He thinks, eyeing it closely. Just then he hears WUKOO! WUKOO! The sound of the space police. 'Oh look, more space police.' He muses with excitement. 'I'll just veer off to this fire planet and…' He trails off as he does exactly that and steers the ship down towards to the fire planet at faster-than-light-speeds (as all spaceships had) with a sharp diagonal turn. He loses the police in the process, but makes quite a crash landing.

Ji climbs out of the rubble from the crash and dusts himself off as he looks around at the newest planet he's landed on.

"Nailed it." He says to himself with a grin, despite the wreck that was his former ship, a ship fit for a king. As he looks around Ji notices a few things. First, the planet was hot, super hot, very much like the magma planet he was on before. Luckily Ji's been done away with his vulnerability to heat or any kind of temperature, having stolen it from himself, but he can tell that if he hadn't he'd be on fire right now and likely turned to ashes by the time he had a chance to scream. Against all possibilities, all laws of physics, and…and *logic* this fire planet, this fire is somehow *hotter* than the magma and lava on the magma planet he left. Which is weird because everyone knows lava is hotter than fire. Then again that's on Earth so maybe things are different elsewhere. With a shrug, Ji continues his observations.

The next thing he notices is that everything on this planet is just like the lavabeasts from the magma planet, the volcanic planet from before. Everything is just fire given shape. The clouds? White fire in the sky given nebulous form. The grass? Green fire that stayed close to the ground and around your feet. The ground? Normal orange-red fire that seemed to have somehow taken a solid form, but is still hot as hell. He could only imagine with the people and animals were like. And the water. Did this planet do the impossible and have water made out of fire? Or maybe they simply lacked water or anything like it. Or maybe it was gasoline, as unsafe as that'd be. He's pretty sure that the air is nothing but gaseous fumes and butane anyhow. Regardless, he had things to explore and treasures to steal, whether they're made of fire or not.

Investigating the planet happened quickly for Ji and he was rapidly becoming an expert in it. After exploring the rest of the world, Ji noted that the water was in fact, NOT gasoline, but some sort of liquid fire that didn't make any kind of scientific sense. The people and animals are essentially the lavabeasts of this world, fire shaped as people and animals, with their own distinct personalities and such. Against all odds, the buildings, roads, and even technology are also made of fire, which just defied all reason. It didn't stop there either; it extended to clothes, vehicles, jewelry, and so on. Literally everything is a form of fire.

Currently, Ji is the heart of the fire kingdom as he calls it, as neither the planet nor the civilizations have any sort of English or human name. He's blending in with the wildlife (what he liked to call the aliens on their planets), the fire people, and is in search of the one treasure that will make this trip worth it. Right now Ji is on one of his last five missions before he moved up a step on the proverbial thieving ladder, and he needed to make these last five count.

After a little sightseeing, he whittled down his choices to only one possible target: the Fire Crystal, a jewel made entirely out of solid fire somehow. He didn't question it anymore given what else he's seen on the planet; instead he buckles down and prepares to infiltrate the armored castle that holds the crystal within it. He moves swiftly, through detection systems and force fields, dodging lasers that try to find his position and fire people that guard the area. The fire people are faster than they look, moving much faster than humans were capable of moving, fast enough to warrant the fire streams they left behind. This makes it slightly more difficult for Ji, but he adjusts quickly to their speed, his hands twitching as he resists simply stealing it from them, and instead makes necessary calculations to continue his quest for the Fire Crystal. Once the alterations to his plan are made, Ji reaches the crystal quickly and is somewhat amazed by what he sees.

The Fire Crystal is...beautiful, awe–inspiring to say the least. The crystal literally takes Ji's breath away as he lays eyes on it. The crystal is shaped like a solidified wisp of flame that is multi-colored, encompassing every color of fire possible, all layered perfectly to create the best aesthetics possible. Slowly Ji reaches out to touch the crystal, still mesmerized by its aura and its beauty. His fingers brush the crystal gently, the sensation being that of extreme heat on a smooth surface that somehow didn't cause pain or harm in any way. Well it wouldn't do much to Ji regardless due to various things stolen from his body, as mentioned before, but he could tell by touching it that it would have the same effect even on normal humans, without his resistance and lack of vulnerabilities. In that way the crystal is extremely special and very unlike the rest of the fire and fire-made things on this planet. It's unique, a treasure, priceless. And now it's his.

Snapping out of his trance, Ji speeds up his movement and hastily snags the crystal and makes his way out of castle and back to his ship. 'Mission success!' Ji thinks to himself in jubilance as he fingers the crystal in his grasp while grinning. After this, there's only five more planets to visit: The Darkness planet, the Light Planet, the Crystal Planet, the Alcohol Planet, and the Gold Planet as he dubbed them, naming them for the substance that the majority of the worlds are made of.

On the Darkness Planet, his target is the Dark Rain, a rare phenomenon where pure darkness burst like a cloud and condensates, forming pure liquid darkness. For the Light Planet, Ji wants to take the special 'galaxy' glass as he calls it. The glass allows all who look through it to see any and every frequency of light, even those normally invisible to the human and alien eye. It also works to identify those who would think themselves invisible or hidden in some way. The Crystal Planet, the Gold Planet, and the Alcohol Planet, have obvious targets: some intergalactic booze, shiny metal, and jewels, all taken from pieces of the planets themselves.

'I wonder if I could've taken her with me on this trip, to bask in my happiness, my glory with me. These are special moments that I'd love to share with her...' He thinks, his thoughts trailing off as he thinks about a certain someone, a childhood friend and Keeper that he left back at home on Earth. 'No, most of these planets are inhabitable by humans and for some of them, the denizens aren't even visible to human sight.' He muses as he decides that he couldn't bring her along with him. 'Add in random extreme temperatures, poisonous air, super strong gravity, super light gravity, and so on and without her being completely initiated into the Keepers, she wouldn't survive without me...stealing from her. And I never steal from her.' He continues his train of thought as he moves throughout the fire kingdom, on his way to find a new ship to steal for further thievery off-planet. 'Not without her permission.' He added. He grins as he finds a military ship made out of solidified fire of some kind, with everything necessary to make it off-world and continue traveling for a while. His hesitance at accepting the logic behind technology made of fire (along with everything else on this world) vanishes the moment he sees the beautiful vessel and his way off the planet and to his other destinations.

With a wide grin, he steps into the military vessel and immediately takes the controls, revving it up for travel and getting it ready for take-off. 'Then again, she could probably go now if she's part of the Keeper Elite.' His thoughts return to Earth and his best friend that he left behind. 'Maybe I just needed to wait a little.' He contemplates. 'Oh well, too late now.' He thinks as he gets the ship into the air and proper position to being his trip.

'Still, would've been nice if she were here.' He thinks as he begins his ride to and throughout space. He coasts for a small moment, feeling out the ship and how it flies, as well as the general motion it takes as it travels throughout hyperspace. 'Let's see if I can make a speed run on these last five.' He says to himself internally as he activates the equivalence of a gear shift on the ship. 'Once I'm done with these, I can move on to bigger and better heights. The moons and the stars. Maybe even literally.' He then shifts the ship down to the next destination of the Darkness Planet.

'Maybe I should let the space police catch me once. Or at least tell them my name and whatnot. That way I can be known as Merc both on Earth and in space.' He thinks with a grin. 'I'll be the greatest thief in not just the world, or the solar system, but the galaxy, and maybe even the universe.' He exclaims excitedly in his head, his grin growing.

"Merc: The Universe's Greatest Thief." He says out loud as he lands on the Darkness Planet. "No, The Greatest Thief in the Universe. Now that has a good ring to it."

CHAPTER ELEVEN

Ji stands on...well it's not clear exactly what he's standing on, but he's outside of his ship, staring at the sight before him: the Crystal Planet. His body is still as he lets the cold of space wash over him, likely immune due to self-thievery, unmoving as he stares ahead. He is bombarded by all sorts of radiation, deprived of any kind of oxygen or breathable air, exposed to deadly elements, and yet...he doesn't care. For what's before him is a beauty unknown to many, something he can't resist due to just how gorgeous, how appealing it is. It is the third most beautiful thing he remembers seeing in his entire life time. And so Ji stands and stares, continuing to do so for some time before he makes his decision. He doesn't just want the treasure of the Crystal Planet, or a piece of it. No, he wants all of it. Just as he took the Seven Wonders of the World, just as he took China and Antarctica, all back on Earth, he is going to take this planet for himself.

'Well the mild peace was nice while it lasted.' He thinks to himself. 'So was fooling around with those space cops.' He then smirks. 'Time to get a little serious, and do my thing. I can see the intergalactic news now: "Planet gone, Merc, strikes again".' And strike he does.

"What do you mean the Crystal Planet is missing?" Exclaims the head of the space police to his communication device built into his helmet, in awe of the news he's hearing. The head of the space police looked much like his men (light armor, a helmet with glass in front to cover the face, lightly armored gauntlets and boots, with an array of guns on a high-tech-looking belt), except where they had white (their armor and gun), he had black. Also his shoulders had extra armor and he had a black cape to go with his ensemble. "What? The Alcohol Planet and the Gold Planet too? Are you kidding me?" He asks, incredulous. "How? What can...? What's happening?" He continues, speaking more to himself than whoever he's communicating with. The head of the police sighs as he responds. "Yeah, I'll see what I can do. Thanks for the information. Over." He says, ending the line of communication. He then sits back and folds his hands, looking down, seemingly in deep thought. Several minutes pass as he murmurs to himself.

"What to do?" He mutters, trying to think. "What *can* we do?" He says out loud as he mentally goes through his options on dealing with what is apparently a thief on an epic scale: planet level to be exact. He shakes his head in frustration. "Nothing really. We can do nothing." He concludes as he takes a deep breath. He then continues thinking aloud. "This...stealing planets? Whole? Without anyone noticing?" He pauses for a moment. "Yeah this is above us. We need to call the Keepers." He concludes with finality.

Two mysterious Keepers with more fancy robes than normal meet together at the Keeper base as they look at Sharia, observing her every move. The two are discussing important matters as they keep an eye on her. A third Keeper, one of the men who recruited Sharia earlier comes up to the two men and speaks.

"She's good." He says quietly. The other two nod in affirmation.

"She's not ready." Says one of the higher-level Keepers.

"She's the only one that can catch him." Counters the Keeper that recruited her.

"Still, we can't just promote her because of that, can we?" Asks the second higher level Keeper. The Keeper that recruited Sharia hesitates before answering, looking reluctant to speak.

"You're right, I guess not. And she can't survive otherwise. It's best...it's best not to tell her then." He concludes.

"My thoughts exactly." Speaks the second higher level Keeper. "But get her fast-tracked on her training. We'll definitely need her in the future and it's not like she doesn't do good work regardless." He commands. The Keeper that recruited Sharia nods in understanding.

"Yes sir, we'll start on that immediately." The second of the higher-level Keepers nods back in response.

"Good. See to it. You are dismissed." He commands as the Keeper that recruited Sharia bows slightly and walks away, leaving the two higher level Keepers to themselves. Once he's gone, the first of the two higher level Keepers talks, addressing the other.

"You say it's best not to tell her about the thief. Why is that? Do you fear that her connection with him will hurt us?" He inquires. The second of the higher-level Keepers shakes his head.

"No, it is not for our well-being that I fear, but for hers. There's a small possibility that she'll actually improve if we tell her, taking it as a challenge or even wanting to see him sooner than later." He begins.

"But..." Beckons the other higher-level Keeper, fishing for answers.

"But it's far more likely for her to shut down even more or start to waver in her work as she'll start to worry for him and his well-being. While I'd love the first situation to occur, we can't afford the realization of second scenario in any capacity. If that happens, we lose not only a good agent and a future Keeper Elite, but we lose our only surefire way to catch this...Merc." He explains. The other higher level Keeper nods.

"I see...it all makes sense then. But for now, we go on with the Keeper Elite, correct?" He questions.

"Correct."

Ji is now in a new location, one not survivable by nearly anything in the universe, so hostile that it can crush a planet just by being in close proximity. With gravity so great and so condensed that it causes time to dilate, as well as immense pressure and heat. Ji is in the middle of a Neutron Star.

"Without all the extreme gravity, pressure, and temperature, this thing's not half bad." Ji says out loud to himself, referring to him stealing the effects of the gravity and pressure from his being so that he could survive being where he is. He looks around with an appreciative grin. "Definitely getting me one. Maybe this one." He adds as an afterthought. Suddenly a sleek black space ship arrives right next to Ji and his possible-neutron-star. The ship is about as large as a city block and has strange symbols on it, carved in black that aren't visible to the naked eye, but are visible to Ji. Thanks to information he stole long ago, Ji knows exactly what, and who this is.

"Huh, Keeper Elites are here." He notices. "Is she...?" Ji wonders out loud, thinking about his childhood friend whom he missed dearly. For a moment his heart jumped and he had a feeling of excitement. But then he uses his unique thieving abilities to peer onto the ship and see who is present. He's a bit disappointed when he doesn't see her, but hope still fills his heart. He then uses the same ability to look for her in particular, and sees that she's in fact on Earth still and not just backup or somewhere in space in pursuit for him. "Nope. Damn." He says to himself, under his breath. Now he is hit with a feeling of immense disappointment, but ultimately shrugs it off. 'Oh well, time to bounce.' He thinks as he waves to the Keeper Elites, still in their ship.

"Nice to see you guys out here!" He yells as he instantaneously disappears, the neutron star going with him. The Keeper Elite in the ship all do a double take at the sight they just beheld. So this was what they were called here for it seemed. One of the Keeper Elite even speaks out loud, voicing the thoughts of everyone.

"What in the...how does he do that?" Asks said Keeper Elite in a distorted voice. Nobody knows outside of Ji himself.

CHAPTER TWELVE

Once again Ji stands outside of his ship, peering deep into endless void of space as he's bombarded by radiation and cold. Like last time, he is looking at a star, but this one is much different than the neutron star he took before. This star is super massive and super-hot, so much so that it is classified as a blue *hypergiant*, the largest and hottest type of all stars. What makes this star even more different is the state the star is in. Currently the star is preparing to explode and go supernova, something which will likely form a black hole due to its size. Or well, it would if Ji wasn't here. And of course, that is what Ji is waiting on, to witness the beauty of nature, of destruction, of the natural life cycle of a star as big, as bright, and as hot as this one. Once it's reached the pinnacle of the explosion, the peak of its beauty, then Ji will step in and do as thieves do. 'Come on, star. Don't make me beg for it.' Ji thinks with a grin. Not a minute after he thinks those thoughts does something happen, something wonderful. BOOM! The hypergiant explodes, finally going supernova. The force, the light, and the heat wash over Ji, his ship, and the entire area for lightyears as the supernova reaches full force, and yet somehow he doesn't flinch or move a muscle. He remains rooted to his spot, merely staring at his prize with a wide grin on his face.

"Wow!" He starts. "It's weird to see how each star explodes differently. A shame this'll be the last of my collection though." He says as he takes the star, mid-supernova, and places it next to the others he's collected in the same state (one of each: a blue giant, blue dwarf, red giant, red supergiant, red hypergiant, yellow hypergiant, white dwarf, yellow giant, white giant, and everything in between). "Had to save the best for last." He muses. 'Or maybe less "best" for last and more "biggest" and "brightest" for last.' He corrects himself in his thoughts. He waits in the outskirts of outer space a while longer, staring at the now empty spot where the star—no, where *his* star used to be. He shakes his head at the craziness of it all and goes back into his ship.

"Next up, a Black hole. And then…a solar system." He says to himself as he re-enters his stolen ship. Before he does much, he looks around as if searching for something. "Keepers seem late." He comments. BOOM! The ship shakes from the attack, causing Ji to grin wildly. "Ah, there they are." He exclaims excitedly as his ship is instantly swarmed and boarded by ten Keeper Elite. The Keeper Elite wear similar robes as normal Keepers, only with different symbols on them. They also wear black masks that have white triangle-shaped glass that extends from the forehead to the mouth. Oh and they also have powerful looking, futuristic guns as weapons, guns they currently have pointed at Ji. In response Ji sighs and puts his hands up in surrender.

"'Sup boys, come to fail at catching me?" He taunts with jubilance. No one talks or responds in any way. Instead they shoot a strange projectile towards Ji, one that looks like a misshapen orb of some strange white energy with a black glow. The orb travels fast, faster than anyone could ever hope to dodge, and hits Ji in the chest, quickly engulfing him until he disappears inside said orb. Unfortunately for the Keeper Elite, Ji pops right back out, reappearing where he once was.

"Was that a pocket dimension?" Questions Ji, incredulous. He knows it was, so it's more of a rhetorical question, one asked in surprise, shock, and awe. "Awesome!" He states, unharmed and unrestrained in anyway by the high-tech attack. "The space cops just had dope lasers with a lot of settings." He muses as he looks up as if trying to remember something. "Hold up let me see if I remember um…" His brow furrows as he concentrates on his memories of the space police. "Paralysis, sleep, stun, burn, freeze, constrict, explode, and kill." He lists off. "Some seem redundant but hey, I didn't design them." He explains with a shrug. The Keeper Elite are not amused. Again, without speaking, they switch their guns to a new setting and fire.

Ten beams hit Ji at once, freezing him solid…for a moment. After the moment is up, Ji steps out of the ice cube somehow (no doubt, due to his aptness at thievery) and comments on the weapon.

"Man, that was cold!" He exclaims. The Keeper Elite tense up at his joking matter and easy survival and escape from that attack. It meant that absolute zero, the temperature at which atoms themselves stopped moving, didn't work on their target. They began to wonder if Merc was impossible to catch. Wiping that thought from their minds, they try to think of ways to take him out. They already knew the gravity functions were useless due to witnessing him standing in the center of a neutron star, and the heat and force functions were useless for much of the same reasons. It looks like they'd have to use their trump card. With a few silent hand signals and nodding from each of them, the Keeper Elite all change their gun to the strongest setting they have and pull the trigger.

Instantly everything around the Keeper Elite stops moving. The ship stops flying through space, air stops circulating through the ship, light from stars stop traveling to the solar systems and planets they shone over, every person not a Keeper Elite stops moving or functioning in any way, and every molecule and atom stops as well. Time and Space itself is frozen. This is the absolute power of the Keeper Elite weapon, to freeze time. Something that no being outside the gods and the Keeper Elite themselves could counter. Or so they hope. They've seen some crazy things over the years, and have seen Merc do the impossible, so nothing is ruled out. Because of this, every one of the Keeper Elite keeps their guns trained on Merc, all moving closer to him slowly, by the inch. It seems to have worked as they get in as close as all ten of them can and still Merc hasn't moved a muscle.

Suddenly Ji moves, holding up his hands as he shouts loudly to surprise the men, as if conducting a high school prank.

"Boo!" He yells, startling the trained elites of the Keepers. Not expecting *any* kind of movement, and being highly trained in ways that no man can imagine, the Keepers Elite respond poorly to the jump scare, and react instantly before they can stop themselves. In one instant, all of their guns simultaneously switch to the most deadly setting: Kill. Pure anti-matter rings out from each of the ten guns and annihilates the ship and everything surrounding it, leaving only the Keeper Elite unscathed.

The Keeper Elite all look at each other and their guns in confusion. What just happened? Did they get him? Did they want to get him like that? The questions travel through the heads of each of the Keeper Elite as they run over the scenario over and over again in their minds. Once they realize what's happened, all of them are surprised at first, mostly at Merc being able to move during the Time Freeze as that's supposed to be impossible, and then they all feel shame and regret. They were supposed to bring the thief in, not kill him. As Elites, it's unacceptable to fail a mission so heavily, even if the target is as dangerous as the thief seemed to be. The Keeper Elite realize that for once in a long time, they may have just messed up.

CHAPTER THIRTEEN

The Keeper Elite return to their ship through the cold, lifeless void of space, somber and silent at the events that had just transpired. A mistake was made, a huge mistake that hasn't been made in a long time, a mistake that couldn't be undone even with all of the advanced technology that the Keepers possessed. With that thought in mind, the Keeper Elite make their way back to Earth, not speaking once the entire way, as they know they'll have a tough explanation to give upon mission report. The Keeper Elite reach the Keeper Headquarters in seemingly no time at all and make their way into the building, slowly, dragging their feet and trying to delay what is to come.

Despite their attempts, the ten Keeper Elite find their way into a large room, each standing in front of the higher-level Keeper that sent them on this mission. The team of men have their weapons sheathed and their heads down as silence takes the room. No one is willing to speak, to volunteer their voice to try to explain he misgivings that passed. The higher-level Keeper can sense the tension in the room. He instantly knows that something is off, the mission went wrong somewhere and no one wants to talk. He sighs deeply and attempts to find out what that is, as he opens his mouth and speaks.

"Keeper Elite, report." He commands in his distorted voice. No one moves to talk. He waits a few more seconds before speaking again. "I notice the thief isn't here, so the mission obviously went wrong somewhere. As Keeper Elite, that is surprising, but I know what you were up against and I won't hold it against you. Failure happens, especially with Merc involved." He explains. "I do need you to speak however as we need to know what happened." The ten Keeper Elite all look at each other, exchanging silent cues to figure out who will be the unlucky person that has to speak. After about ten seconds of motioning, one of the Keeper Elite sits up and answers.

"Sir, we located the target in a far-off system, the Sephiroth system, where a blue hypergiant was going supernova." Begins the Keeper Elite in a voice that's even more distorted than the Keeper norm. "From our intel, the thief was collecting all types of supernovas, one of each kind of star, and this was the last one he needed: the biggest and hottest of all stars." He explains, hesitating for a moment.

"And this is where the mission went wrong?" Asks the higher-level Keeper, leaning forward in intrigue. The Keeper Elite shakes his head.

"No, not yet. I was just gathering myself sir, my apologies." He responds. "By the time we reached the area, the star was already gone and the thief had already made it back to his ship. We boarded his ship immediately, excited to have finally caught this...aberration that we were trailing as he had lost us every other time, taunting us as he escaped." Describes the Keeper Elite as the higher-level Keeper looks on in interest.

"I see, and then?" Prompts the higher-level Keeper.

"Then we followed protocol as normal, with a little overkill. First we tried to capture him with ten simultaneous pocket dimensions folded onto one another. He broke out." This startles the higher-level Keeper as he jumps in his chair a bit.

"He what? That's impossible!" Exclaims said Keeper, as the Keeper Elite shakes his head in response.

"That's what we thought too. Even one of those is supposed to be impossible, but ten? Nothing less than the gods could even hope to contend. And yet, he escaped. Seeing what we were up against, we all began wracking out brains for a solution, and being as coordinated as we are, we all went for the absolute zero beams. All ten of us simultaneously." He pauses for a bit, as if thinking it over. "He broke out of that too. Seemingly stepping out of the frozen block that held him. It didn't make any sense to us." The higher-level Keeper nods in understanding. He too couldn't comprehend how someone could simply ignore absolute zero.

"I see…is this when he escaped then?" Inquires the higher-level Keeper, still in shock at the tale of the impossible escapes orchestrated by the thief in question. The Keeper Elite shakes his head in denial of said statement.

"No, unfortunately…no. From there we had to think once more on what to do. We knew that the gravity setting wouldn't do anything as last time we saw him, he was standing in the middle of a neutron star, unscathed."

"A neutron star?" Asks the higher-level Keeper, incredulous. The Keeper Elite only nods.

"This also ruled out the heat setting on our weapons and the force setting as well." He then takes a deep breath, heard through his head piece. "So we decided to use the Time Freeze setting. If he could get past absolute zero and a pocket dimension, it was the only option." The Keeper Elite speaks in a more somber tone.

"And he escaped this as well?" Says the higher-level Keeper in disbelief. The Keeper Elite nods once more.

"Yes, that…that is where the problem lies." Speaks the Keeper Elite. The higher-level Keeper shakes his head.

"No, you can't blame yourselves for that. This…thief appears to have extraordinary abilities that exceed time itself. Him escaping isn't a slight on you. If he's capable of that, then no one—"

"It's not just that he escaped." Explains the Keeper Elite, cutting off the higher-level Keeper, causing him to close his mouth and nod, waiting to hear the rest. "I…we…didn't expect him to be moving during the Time Freeze. *Nothing* is supposed to be moving during the Time Freeze, except us. And yet…he jumped out and he scared us." He stops to swallow. "And we killed him."

"You…you what?" Questions the higher-level Keeper in shock.

"He jumped, we jumped too. Only our jumper involves an itchy trigger finger and the deadliest training in the world, as you know. We all had the same reflex: switch to the Anti-Matter setting and blast. Nothing was left, not even his ship." He says the last part quietly, looking down. The rest of the Keeper Elite also look down when he mentions it. The higher-level Keeper brings his hands up to his mouth.

"I see...so the thief...is dead." He says aloud to himself. He then sighs as he lies back in his chair. "This...could be a problem." Silence reigns once more as he sits back and thinks. "Not with what you did, I'm referring to someone else." He speaks, thinking about Sharia. "There's nothing wrong with what you did, and I understand your trepidation, I really do. You haven't failed anything in a while and it was jarring to be forced into a mistake by the very target you were after." He explains. "It's rare for agents on your level, but it happens. Sleep it off and you'll recover." He states confidently. "You're dismissed."

The Keeper Elite nod towards him and all exit the room, eager to get out of there. As they leave, the higher-level Keeper sits back and ponders Sharia and how she'll handle this. More importantly, he ponders how he'll handle her. His eyes immediately drawn to her as she moves through the facility and he can only look at her with pity as he thinks of the situation: Her very own employer killed her best friend. Tragic.

A month passes before the Keepers work up the nerve to tell Sharia. First the higher-level Keeper deigns to keep the information to himself, but eventually as time passes, he opts to share the information with other higher ups in the Keeper organization. The information continues to travel and eventually it makes its way to the two Keepers who recruited Sharia in the first place. Both Keepers feel responsible for Sharia and feel that they have an obligation to tell her. So at the start of the first month, the two call her into a random room and ask her to take a seat.

"Sharia, we wish we didn't have to have this conversation, and I'll say ahead of time that I'm sorry." Speaks the first of the two Keepers. This confuses Sharia.

"Sorry? For what exactly?" She asks, unsure of what's going on.

"It's about Merc." Starts the second Keeper. This causes Sharia's heart to jump in excitement and then drop as it likely means something is wrong with him.

"M...Merc?" She asks, feeling her lips get dry as she gets nervous at what the news can possibly be. The second Keeper nods.

"Yes, we know you had some kind of relationship with him. It seemed you two were close." Explains the Keeper. Sharia nods, feeling her throat tightening up as she notices that the Keeper is referring to Ji in the past tense.

"What happened?" She asks, forcing her voice not to waver or falter. The first Keeper looks at her in pity as he cuts in.

"Last month Merc had a run in with the Keeper Elite due to some...problems he was causing. His stealing had evolved to a whole 'nother scale." He stops to swallow. "During his encounter, he escaped from several of their most advanced constraints, pocket dimensions, and time freeze among them, but...he also managed to scare the Keeper Elite in the process and...they got jumpy..." He trails off.

"And what?" Questions Sharia, fearful of what the answer might be. She tries to wipe the fear out her mind as she thinks on all the impossible things Ji has done. She knows he's alive and can survive anything. She just knows it. The first Keeper's shoulders drop as he responds.

"Anti-Matter." He whispers out. Her heart sinks, like a rock, all the way to the core of the Earth and beyond, going on for eternity. Anti-Matter was...overkill. Nothing can survive it. Literally. Luckily she's already sitting down as her legs feel weak, wobbly, and her vision starts to blur, becoming unfocused. Despite her grief, she doesn't cry. She's just...empty. Numb. Thinking about how she'll never see him again and how she never even got a chance to say goodbye. She waits there, staring into the ether for what seems like eons before she comes to her senses and realizes that the two Keepers are waiting for her, concerned about how she'll take the news. She tries to force a smile, but she just...can't. Instead she nods solemnly and addresses both men.

"Thank you for letting me know." She says rather emotionlessly as she gets up and walks out of the room, and out of the facility. She just...needed to get away. The numbness doesn't go away on her trip home, or even when she opens the door to her house. She walks into her house, trying to act normally, as if she had just come home from work, but finds herself moving in slow motion, as if trying to wade through molasses. Somehow she can't get herself to care however as she's still empty from the news on Ji. Many hours later, once she's done with cleaning up, with cooking, with everything that needs to be done, she sits down on her bed and stares into the ether as she thinks of him. Still she doesn't cry, still she doesn't feel emotion, still she can't focus. It's too devastating.

As time passes, wounds heal. That is the natural flow of life. With those words and that idea in mind, Sharia returns to work the next day, and the day after that, and the day after that as well, and so on. Each day she works mindlessly, lifelessly, yet efficient, as she thinks about what could've been. Sometimes the thoughts were fantasies of Ji returning, dumb grin on his face and arms wide open, to show her that he's fine. Other times, the fantasies have her running off with him and abandoning her duties as a Keeper in the process. On occasion, she even sees various points in her past where she chooses to go with him instead of fight him, and then they live in harmony forever. It is not lost on her that in none of these realities, even in her own mind, is he not a thief.

At the end of each of these days, she performs the same ritual from the first day of getting home, eating, cleaning, and performing other chores, before she sits down on her bed and stares into the ether. No matter how many days pass, the feelings inside of her remain the same as always, and she doesn't recover one bit. As more time passes, she even gets through her first Movie Night without him. She tries to set up everything: the snacks, the pajamas, the movie, the blankets, but when he doesn't show she ends up feeling emotion for the first time. The emotion in question? Depression. She's not able to finish the movie she picked and instead goes to sit on her bed and stare, like she always did after work. The other Movie Nights went the same, except she skips the setup part and taps right into the depression, sleeping the day away.

"Sir, check this report." Says a random Keeper as he hands a sheet of paper to the higher-level Keeper who commands the Keeper Elite. The higher-level Keeper looks over the document in shock and surprise as it details the impossible.

"Black holes being taken? Super massive black holes as well? Hypernovas, solar systems used like trinkets, and an entire galaxy disappearing out of nowhere." He murmurs to himself as he reads the full story on the paper before him. 'This is impossible.' He thinks to himself. 'That man is dead.'

"Is it him, sir?" Asks the random Keeper, snapping the higher-level Keeper out of his self-induced trance.

"Is it who, agent?" Inquires the higher-level Keeper.

"Him. Merc. He's the only one who could—" Begins the random Keeper, trying to explain his stance. The higher-level Keeper merely raises his hand, stopping him mid-sentence.

"Does it matter, agent? At this point, this is something we can't handle. We're good, the best even. But we can't handle a man who can take an entire galaxy on a whim. Only the gods can handle someone on this level." He says truthfully. For Sharia's sake, he actually wishes that it is Merc. She's been excellent in her job lately, acing every assignment, topping her class in all of her training, but he could see that the death of her friend was heavily affecting her. She'd given them so much with her good work and they'd only taken from her, taken the most important person in her life. It doesn't seem like a fair trade. He knows she'll get over it eventually, but the healing process is moving at a snail's pace. If this turns out to be Merc, maybe she'll finally feel happiness again and he can rid himself of the guilt he feels. Just maybe.

Weeks pass until one day, Sharia gets an assignment from her new boss, the higher-level Keeper. There's a phenomenon on Earth, one that ranks above normal Keepers. That's not what bothers her however. What bothers her is the location of the phenomenon: the old park where she and Ji used to hang out. The park brings back painful memories and she's forced to move her thoughts to him as she wonders just how long it's been without him. 'It's been a year now.' She thinks to herself, very unwilling to go to back to that place. 'And just when I'd made some progress too.' She says internally, referring to her no longer staring into the ether every day as she got home from work.

She arrives at the destination quickly and stops as she sees the issue. There's a strange white mass at the park, located right in the place that she and Ji called their own. With a deep breath to calm her nerves, she makes her way towards the white mass, ready for action. As a Keeper Elite, she shouldn't be scared as very little can hurt her, but it doesn't help that she can't seem to get any readings on this phenomenon through her mask or her gun. Because of that, this is completely uncharted territory and completely unsafe. It's the unknown. But this is her job now as a Keeper Elite, to handle exactly that. On guard, she steps into the white mass and there she sees a figure. She gets closer to the figure to try and get a good look. As she gets within ten feet of the figure, she finally sees it clearly. What she sees...cannot be. The very sight ceases her body and mind as she drops her gun to the floor and must do everything within her power not to suffer the same fate.

CHAPTER FOURTEEN

Sharia is speechless at the sight before her. Inside she's screaming at herself repeatedly in the most wicked of voices. 'This can't be real! This can't be!' Say the voices, loud in her head, thick with denial. Suddenly she gets paranoid and starts looking around to see what exactly *is* this white mass. 'What's in here?' She wonders. As far as she can tell, it was nothingness, just…white. At this moment, the figure turns around and waves, speaking as he does.

"Hey." Says Ji nonchalantly.

"Hey? I thought you were…" She rages initially before calming down and stepping forward to give him a big hug, wrapping her arms around him as tight as she can, intent on never letting go. Ji returns the hug as he somehow knows exactly what she thought about him due to her reaction to seeing him. He knows that normally she'd be happy to see him, but never *this* happy. Also her words from earlier tip him off. After what feels like an eternity, in a good way, Sharia finally pulls back from the hug a bit as she asks the question that's nagging her mind. "Where are we?" Ji shrugs as he answers.

"A white hole." He says. "Can't be penetrated from the outside by…well anything. Matter can escape once it's inside though. Think of like an anti-black hole." He explains.

"Oh." She says in comprehension. "Then how did I—?"

"Because I let you." He answers with a smile, not at all bothered by her deeply distorted voice. She nods in understanding before she speaks once more.

"It's so bleak, colorless." She says softly, hinting something to her returned friend.

"Yeah." He whispers back as he gets the clue and lets light in so they can see their surroundings, the scenic field that they always loved as kids.

"How?" She asks, but his shushes her, putting his finger to her mask.

"Your turn." He says, causing her to nod and remove her mask and her robes. "There it is. The beautiful face I was missing all this time." He finishes, causing her to blush.

"I missed you too, Ji." She replies, finally using her normal voice.

"Ah, and the melodic voice too." He says, teasing her. This causes her to smile as she finally has him back. Back from his adventures in outer space, back from death.

"You know Sharia, despite me being a thief...between the two of us, it's you who's stolen from me." He begins softly. Sharia looks taken aback as she tries to think of what he could be talking about. She hates stealing. She'd never...she trails off and instead realizes he's playing a game of sorts and decides to play along.

"Really? And what have I stolen from you, Ji?" She questions with a soft tone as well.

"Just one thing: my heart." He replies with a smile. "And I want to do the same to you." He says as he stops and thinks about it. "But not like that." He corrects himself seeing as he's an actual thief and his words can be misinterpreted. "I don't want your actual heart, and I don't to...steal it per say, but I want you to feel for me, like I do for you." He explains as he grabs her hands and holds them to his lips. She blushes hard as she takes in his words, her heart jumping as she hears words that are like music to her ears. All of the numbness, all of the pain is gone and now it is replaced by only elation!

"Ohiji Olezuo." She begins in a doting tone. "Of course I feel the same way. I always have I guess, I just never..."She trails off not knowing how to say it. His smile lets her know that she doesn't have to.

"You know it's supposed to rain today Shar." He says suddenly, almost changing the subject. "But I stole the rain from the clouds, so we could have this moment in this perfect weather. Sharia looks at him, bewildered by such an action. Keeper Elite or not, stealing rain from the clouds just didn't make sense. "Let me show you." He says as he opens his right hand

and the clouds suddenly get gray and rain showers come down. She looks up in awe, never having seen anything like this before first hand and wonders aloud as she looks around.

"Is this some kind of illusion?" She speaks under her breath? Apparently, Ji hears her though as he shakes his head and lets the rain through the white hole, as the water hits them both.

"Just say when." He commands her. She nods as she thinks about everything for a while, how crazy it is to have Ji back and to finally see...what he does up close. It's so amazing that she doesn't even care about getting wet. Eager to test something, she speaks.

"When." And it all stops immediately, the rain and the effect of the rain on her hair and her clothes, as she's no longer wet.

"No matter how honored I am that you got wet for me, I did you a solid and took the rain back in totality, from the sky and from your body." He explains, causing her to blush at the innuendo he purposely put in there. At the same time, she's in awe of his...abilities. She didn't know what to think when she heard that he'd stolen Las Vegas or Hawaii or China or Antarctica, or even when he stole all money and weapons from the planet. She just kind of assumed he'd performed a very intricate job of some sorts, and nothing really made sense to her even when they explained it. During her entire time in the Keeper's organization, she always wondered how Ji qualified as something they would hunt, an aberration, an anomaly who broke the rules of reality. But now, after seeing that, she understands.

"Are you a god Ji? Or some kind of supernatural being? The things you do...they don't make sense." She asks out loud, causing Ji to shake his head.

"No, I'm just a thief Shar. And really good at it." He explains. "Watch." He commands as he points up to a cloud. "Look at that cloud." He says. Sharia's eyes follow as she does what he says. "Now blink." He says. She does, and suddenly the cloud's gone. "Now continue staring in that spot." He instructs her. She nods and complies, staring hard as suddenly the cloud appears again. "Voila!" He says with a grin.

"That...that's amazing." She says, in awe.

"I am the Greatest Thief in the Universe, remember?" He reminds her with a cocky tone. "I can take or put back anything I want. I don't believe in limits Shar, and have long stolen them from myself, so nothing is impossible." He says as he looks down at her. "Especially with you by my side." He all-but-whispers the last part, taking in her appearance as he basks in her presence, a presence he longed for the entire year he was gone. "The light of the sun pales in comparison to your beauty, to your brilliance, Sharia. And I'll prove it." He says softly as suddenly everything turns dark on the entire planet. Sharia is wowed by the display and touched by his words as she looks lovingly into Ji's eyes, somehow still able to see him.

"Anything that I want is mine." He explains. "Or yours should you request it."

"And with all of this, you've never taken *anything* from me? Anything at all?" She asks, remembering his previous words and promise towards her. He shakes his head no.

"Death, pain, suffering, the ability to be harmed. Sadness, despair, maybe your own personal limits. These are the only things I'd ever take from you." He describes in a low voice as she nods in understanding. "But I haven't. Not until you say when." He whispers as he gets close, within millimeters of her lips. Sharia closes her eyes and leans in when BANG! Suddenly lightning hits, descending from the heavens themselves as both are hit. Ji is fine, unharmed from the attack as he stole his own mortality from himself long ago, but Sharia is not. Despite being a Keeper Elite and immune to most forms of damage, she still hurt from the lightning attack, and badly at that. Ji's mind is numb as he tries to think on what could've happened. 'We were in a white hole! Nothing can penetrate that! Only the gods themselves...' His thoughts trail off as he realizes what's happened. Like the Keepers before them, the gods were after him. 'If they want me, then they'll get me.' He thinks as he cradles Sharia in his arms, worried about her health. In an instant, a beam of light shoots down from the sky and brings Ji to the heavens themselves, with Sharia in his arms.

CHAPTER FIFTEEN

His body hunched over Sharia's, Ji lifts his head somewhat in order to look around and get a sense of his surroundings. It appears that he's in an area of pure divine energy, where the ground itself is made of the clouds while the surrounding walls are made of a gold substance. He continues to look and notices that he is front of an audience, made of the gods themselves. The gods by nature are in a form that is not perceivable by the mortal eye. If glanced upon by a normal man or woman, said man or woman would instantly fall into insanity and never recover for they have seen something their mind cannot comprehend. Ji however is anything but a normal mortal man and has stolen such limitations from his eyes and his mind long ago. Instead of going crazy, Ji sees their forms, very humanoid in nature with dark skin and divine energy as robes, and is merely intrigued by the situation— or he would be if Sharia wasn't hurt at the moment. 'They're gods. They can help. They can fix her.' He thinks as he goes to open his mouth. He's cut off by the one of the gods beating him to it.

"Ohiji Olezuo, you have been judged by the gods and we have found your actions...displeasing." Comes the booming divine voice that is heard on all levels of existence, whether it's physical, mental, spiritual, metaphysical, and so on.

"You have dared to violate the laws of what should be and shed your limitations. You have stolen that which shouldn't be stolen and now you shall be punished!" States the voice of a different god, albeit with the same properties.

"You—"

"I don't care." Interrupts Ji, as he looks back down at Sharia's prone body. "Just...fix it. Fix her. She has nothing to do with this." He demands.

"You DARE!" Yells, the god that he cut off, enraged at his show of disrespect. Ji stays where he is, unwavering and unafraid, only determined and worried for Sharia's health.

"I do. Now please, just fix her." He pleads this time, his voice betraying his desperation.

"We shall not." Answers a different god. **"She is simply collateral damage in *your* punishment. A symptom of *your* transgressions, of *your* crimes."** Ji starts shaking as he tries to keep himself from crying, from showing weakness.

"Fine." He starts, softly. "I'll give up stealing, put everything back to the way it's supposed to be, and do whatever you want. Just please, fix her!" He yells, tears streaming down his face as he can no longer hold in his feelings. The gods are unimpressed and unmoving in their thoughts.

"No." Comes yet another divine voice. **"Consider this part of your punishment."** Speaks the voice with conviction.

"Besides," Begins another of the gods. **"This is the work of the God of Destruction. So even if we wanted to, it'd be…difficult so say the least to undo the destruction from destruction incarnate."** The divine being explains. Ji tries unsuccessfully to stop crying as he croaks out his next words.

"She's dying." His voice cracking with emotion.

"And?" Asks one of the divine beings, not caring much for a mere mortal, even if they are a Keeper Elite. Ji takes the time to dry his tears and whisper the statement one more time, more to himself than anyone else.

"She's dying." His eyes then steel over. "No more." He states in a serious voice. "Until I can heal her…until she says when…I…I have to make sure she survives." He says out loud to himself. He then looks towards the gods with a determined look. "This is on you." He states matter-of-factly.

"Mortal, what are you—" The divine voice stops as Ji has suddenly disappeared.

"What did he mean?" Asks one of the other gods.

"He's taken it. Time." Speaks a third god, confusing the other divine beings until they realize what that meant. Ji has stolen all of time, leaving everything frozen besides himself and the gods (due to them being abstract concepts and beings).

Ji find the Destruction God in an instance by using the information he stole from the other gods. Without fear, Ji steps forward, ready to confront the god about fixing what he'd done to Sharia.

"Destruction god." Ji addresses him in a serious tone. "You *will* fix what you've done and heal Sharia." He commands the divine being. The Destruction God, dressed in divine energy shaped as a red karate gi, with an afro for his hair, laughs at Ji's audacity, even taunting him in the process.

"Hahahahahaha! Are you serious mortal? You wish to command me? The God of Destruction? And for what? To heal your mortal *whore*?" Ji's eyes turn downright malevolent at the slight towards Sharia and his face contorts.

"I don't kill, or even like to harm others usually." He says simply as he breathes in and out deeply. "But I no longer have my morals, my humanity. Not for—not right now. So I would tread carefully." He warns the divine being. Again the Destruction God taunts him.

"Am I supposed to be scared? I am a god of the highest order, and you are nothing but a mortal!" States the god with a spiteful tone. In that moment, Ji immediately steals the Destruction God's heart, holding it in his hand. The god of destruction's eyes widen in surprise right Ji crushes it, bringing the divine being to one knee, seriously hurt. Ji doesn't stop his assault however and takes his right eye next, crushing that in his hand as well, forcing the god to try to cover his empty socket with his own hand and flinch from the pain. Next Ji steals the gods' balls, as he's taken on the form of a man, and holds them in his hand as he grins menacingly.

"It's rather fitting." Ji says in a sadistic voice. "You didn't have the balls to fight me man to man after all. You instead chose to sneak attack me, the very action that got her hurt in the first place!" He exclaims as he crushes said balls in his hand, causing immense amounts of pain and agony to the divine being who thought himself invincible. The god shivers in pain and is introduced to it once more as his right arm is ripped from his body, Ji taking it and throwing it away, and then his brain is taken as Ji stomps on it with malice.

"You deserve this you weak god! You did this to her! You killed her! And I will do the same to you." Yells Ji angrily. The destruction god sneers at the insult and gathers his divine powers, ready to do battle.

"You presume too much human. I am a god, and thus I do not die from wounds like these. My very essence is immortal in all ways!" He shouts as he stands once more. The Destruction God doesn't wait for a reply and instead shoots out a destructive fire, the very fire that will consume the universe at the end of its life, towards his opponent. Ji doesn't move an inch and instead steals both the heat and the destructive aspect of the fire, suffering no damage whatsoever.

"As I said, weak. I easily stole the heat and destruction from your attack and stand here unharmed." This angers the Destruction God who attacks once more, this time with powerful divine wind. Again, the attack does nothing as Ji merely steals the speed from the winds as well as the destructive force once again. "And this time, I stole the very speed from your winds. Do you have anything better?" He taunts with a sneer.

The god of destruction is now livid and tries to hit Ji with pure destructive force, impact incarnate, but this time the thief steals his own ability to be harmed. The force washes over Ji and he remains stable, unmoving from the attack. The Destruction God gets desperate and tries pure destructive energy this time, literal destruction incarnate, able to destroy anything in its path. Ji stares down the attack and steals its ability to do harm. He then quickly does the same to the god, rendering him unable to attack any further.

"How pathetic, a Destruction God who can destroy nothing." Taunts Ji with malice as he finishes the job, taking the god of destruction's powers away. As he does this, the Destruction God looks down at his hands in disbelief, feeling his lack of power, something that is unfamiliar to him.

"Please, give them back! Give me back my powers! I beg of you!" Pleads the former Destruction God, no longer having his divine aura.

"Bring her back. And then we can talk." Counters Ji without emotion, without care. The former god looks lost at that answer. His mouth opens and closes several times like a fish, before he finally answers in a timid voice.

"I...I can't. I can only destroy on that level, not heal. I...I can't help her." He admits quietly. Ji is silent as he contemplates his next move. Unfortunately for the former god, Ji is without his humanity so his next decision is ruthless. Without a care, Ji takes his immortality and the former dies, succumbing to his wounds.

Ji returns his own humanity and immediately returns to the gods, startling them. The gods jump in surprise and a little bit of fear as they can sense the death of their fellow immortal, the god of destruction. They all stare at him, waiting for him to speak, and he obliges them.

"How do I save her?" He asks bluntly. The gods are stumped, unable to answer with any kind of certainty. One of the gods does take a stab at the answer however.

"You mean without stealing from her. Stealing something like her—"

"Which we've established that I won't." The god is cut off by Ji who interrupts him in an irritated tone. The god continues, ignoring the slight for the time being.

"Then you'd need to somehow heal destruction wrought by destruction incarnate." Answers the god. Ji gives said god a pointed look, asking the divine being to continue. Instead the other gods answer for him.

"That is impossible."

"No one can do that."

"Only the Creator can do such a thing."

"The Creator himself would have to bless her." Come the responses rapidly. Ji nods in understanding.

"So the Creator can do it? Then I will speak to him." States Ji as he readies himself to leave. "Where is he?" Asks Ji, realizing he doesn't know the first thing about reaching said Creator. The gods all hesitate to answer, caught between their fear of Ji and their fear of the Creator. Ji loses his patience with them as they continue to be silent. "WHERE!" He yells in agitation and anger. The gods cower slightly before one, a woman stands up and speaks.

"The Creator is not to be bothered. His wrath is great and his power infinite." She states matter-of-factly.

"I didn't ask that." Voices Ji coldly. "Where. Is. He!?" Asks Ji once more, accentuating each word as his agitation grows. The gods grow silent once more, contemplating their next move. Again the same goddess from before steps forward to speak, wary of giving Ji any information, in fear of the Creator's wrath.

"I—" She begins, but is cut off before she can utter more than a single syllable.

"In his realm. Got it." Says Ji, stealing the knowledge from her and the heads of the other gods. "So he has heralds..." Ji trails off, processing said information. The gods look at each other, worried of what the Creator's response might be. And so the gods step forward in an attempt to stop Ji from leaving, from disturbing the Creator.

CHAPTER SIXTEEN

"Stop!" Exclaims the same goddess from before, a beautiful woman covered in exotic robes made of divine energy. Her hair is long, black, and braided and is shaped like a dream catcher as it sticks out behind her head.

"We can't let you go." Exclaims a male god, the first god to speak to Ji when he was brought to the heavens. **"If we did, He'd take his wrath out on us."** He explains. Ji stops mid-step as he turns to the gods, eyes filled with irritation.

"I don't hold as big a grudge against you, as I do—did the Destruction God, so I won't kill you. But if you stand in my way, I won't have much mercy." He states with a cold voice. The gods all hesitate as they know exactly what Ji can do. However his power pales in comparison to the Creator in their mind, so they know what they must do, albeit reluctantly. They must stop him at all costs. Tension fills the air as Ji stares down the gods themselves, those who would stop him in his quest to save Sharia's life. To say the least, he is not amused. A battle is brewing and both sides can feel it, though only one side is overly concerned with the outcome. Because of this, it is a long while before any of the gods step forward, though the first to do so is who else, but the god of speed.

The god of speed rushes Ji at impossible velocities, moving so fast he is everywhere at once, wanting to bombard Ji with force that will smite him into dust. Ji however counters by snapping his fingers and stealing the god's speed, leaving him powerless. The god stops mid charge and falls over, sick from the feeling, as he curls up in a fetal position as he is without his very essence.

"Ironic isn't it. I was named Merc, which is short for Mercury, after the Roman God of Speed. Yet here I face the *actual* god of speed, basically the real Mercury, and *I* am quicker on the draw. Perhaps you should be named after me." Ji muses. As he does, he is attacked by the same goddess from before, the god of magic.

The god of magic immediately weaves a multitude of spells simultaneously, trying to find any possible weakness in the Universe's Greatest Thief. The first of the spells attempts to turn Ji into stone, while the second attempts to bind him and seal him into an infinite dimension of holding. Both fail as Ji steals the ability for magic to affect him. She does not give up however and tries warping reality itself, affecting Ji's destiny, his future, his past, and even removing his ability to steal from him. She tries turning him into stone, a sleep spell, and even an unbreakable wall to block his path, but all fail as he sighs and the wall disappears. Before she can do anything else, Ji steals her ability to do magic, ending the fight and causing her eyes to widen in shock.

"You…how?" She exclaims as she falls to her knees and hangs her head. **"Creator, I have failed you."** She murmurs to herself. As she accepts defeat, another goddess steps up. This goddess is dressed in armored robes and has her hair tied up in a black bun. She is the god of victory.

"I am the God of Victory, thief. Give up! By definition I cannot lose." She proclaims. Ji shrugs and snaps his fingers.

"And now neither can I." He snaps his finger again. "And now, you can't win." He states, as she backs away in fear, feeling his words to be true.

"I…you can override my divinity? The domain over which I rule? You can deny Victory itself?" She cries out, incredulous at the events that just took place. Ji shrugs once more.

"I guess I can." As soon as he says that, another goddess, one with paler brown skin that is almost a grey color, with no hair, dressed in a dull white hooded robe touches his shoulder from behind. She is the god of death. White divine energy pours from her body as Death itself wraps itself around Ji, trying to snuff his life from existence. Ji yawns as it does, not the least bit worried, and casually steals her ability to kill. He addresses her with a shrug as she looks down at her hands in surprise, recoiling from him when he took her powers.

"I took my own mortality long ago. I can't die. That makes you useless against me. And now, you can't kill, so you're useless against everyone." He explains in a bored tone. "Now is that it or—?"

"Come face me in battle if you dare! All who test my sword, shall perish!" Ji is interrupted by a large man with locs on his head, a long beard, a mustache, and divine energy in the shape of heavy armor on his body. This is the god of war. Ji stares at the man who interrupted him and cocks an eyebrow.

"Did you not hear me? I can't die. So anything you do is worthless—"

"We shall see about that, mortal scum!" Exclaims the God of War as he tries to rush Ji at superluminal speeds with his godly blade in his hand. Ji doesn't even flinch as he steals the War God's speed mid-charge, not allowing him to even move, and steals his sword as well for good measure. Ji holds the blade in his hand and feels the tip of the blade with pointer finger.

"Impressive blade, impossibly sharp, but still useless against me." He says as the sword disappears from his hands. "Though I am a thief at heart, so it stays with me." The god of war internally shakes in anger at his sword being taken, but is unable to move to do anything about it. Ji notices the struggle and gives a cocky smirk. "Oh yeah, you still can't move. Here, have your speed back." He speaks, somewhat enjoying himself. The War God grits his teeth and tries to attack once more, this time with a punch. BOOM! The punch lands on Ji's face, though he's unaffected by the blow, having stolen the strength from the punch long before it connected. The War God tries another punch, and this time Ji steals his durability, causing him to break his hand on impact. The god of war jumps back, howling as he holds his hand in pain.

"You! I will end you with an arrow to the heart!" He spits out angrily. Ji grins at those words.

"A good idea, let's see how you fair." He says as he suddenly has a godly bow in his hands, nocks an arrow from the god of war's own armory, steals his own ability to miss, and aims for the War God's heart as he lets said arrow go. The War God's eyes widen as he's hit by the godly arrow and brought to his knees by his own weapon. Before Ji or the god of war can make another move, another god steps up, this one dressed in golden robes with a strange hat on his head, and a black clock hanging around his neck. He lacks any facial hair and looks serious and ready to go. He is the god of time.

"Stop!" Yells the Time God, exerting his power over not just normal time, but the time of the immortals as he tries to freeze Ji in place and trap him in time. Ji raises and eyebrow and dispels the god's hopes with one simple word.

"Nah." The god of time doesn't take kindly to the resistance put forth and tries to age Ji first forward in time until his death, and then back in time until before his birth. Neither work. The god then tries a different strategy and tries to force Ji through time itself, sending him to the future, the past, and all sorts of times in between. Again it doesn't work and Ji stays rooted. **'Why won't this work?'** Wonders the Time God to himself, as he exerts the full might of his powers. Ji simply sighs and snaps his finger, stealing all of time itself, making the Time God useless.

"Now what do you rule over? Nothing." Says Ji with a sneer as he awaits his next divine challenger. Like clockwork, another goddess steps up, this one with long braided hair and dressed in long flowing silver robes. She is the god of Space.

"You guys don't quit." Ji states in a bored tone, becoming more serious again as he calms down from his spat with the War God. The Space God tries her hand at stopping the Greatest Thief in the Universe, folding space itself around him, and even trapping him in an infinitely folding dimension that allows no escape. Until now, when Ji escapes it and snaps, stealing Space itself. "And now you're like your brother." He states, referring to the sister-brother relationship of space and time. "Powerless."

The god of fate is next, an exotically beautiful woman with an afro, wearing a black and red dress. The Fate Goddess tries to manipulate his essence, his future decisions, his luck, and so on, but Ji merely steals his own bad luck and his ability to perform and make bad decisions.

This leaves Fate powerless against him. At the same time the god of sleep, a man with a long beard and long braided hair, wearing blue robes, steps up and tries to force Ji to sleep, using his divine influence.

"**Sleep, mortal.**" He commands in a hypnotic voice that works without fail. Unfortunately there is a first time for everything as Ji merely steals the ability to go to sleep from himself.

"I'm good actually, thanks." He replies as he turns to his next challenger, a gorgeous woman in red with her hair done in curls wearing a seductive red dress. She walks up to Ji slowly in a graceful manner as he keeps his eyes trained on her, as if in a trance.

"**Ohiji Olezuo.**" She says softly in an enticing tone. "**You can defeat any force in the universe, but not that which you fight for.**" She says as she is now right next to him, circling him like an animal circling its prey. "**For if you do, then your entire purpose for being here is gone.**" She says softly, as Ji's eyes continue to follow her movements. "**You cannot defeat Love.**" Speaks the god of love herself, as she tries to influence Ji to give up, to leave the heavens and instead spend time with Sharia in her last few moments she has left. Ji takes a deep breath as he responds to her.

"I can and I did." He says, referring to her last statement. "You have no hold on me." This causes the Love God to recoil in surprise as none have resisted her so, especially none that were in love. "It was a fine try though." He remarks.

"**I see…then perhaps you will fare better without me and my forces.**" She states as she tries to sap the love from his body, and thus his reason to want to see the Creator. Ji grins in response.

"Nah, I'm good as I am. I'd prefer to keep my love as it is, so back off before I go on the offense." He warns the Love God. She does as he says, seeing that it's a fight she can't win, allowing the god of wisdom to step forward, a man dressed in black robes with no hair on his head, but a heavy braided beard and mustache combination. Before the Wisdom God can use his vast intelligence to try to figure out a way to stop Ji, Ji strikes first and simply steals his wisdom from him, ending their conflict before it begins. He then turns and does the same to the god of power, a man with a large afro and no hair on his face, dressed in divine energy shaped as pants on his legs, boots on his feet, and gloves on his hands.

As Ji takes his power, he feels something that he's never felt before: a feeling of invigoration from the power. The power he has is above the power he experienced from the other gods by a large margin. Even the Destruction God paled in comparison as far as raw power goes. Ji basks in the power for a little while before letting it go (not back to the Power God however) as it's not his thing to be immensely powerful. He's a thief and nothing more. Ji scans over the gods and sees dozens of other gods looking on hesitantly, unsure if they should challenge him as well. He steals their emotions and sees that they're fearful of truly stepping up as none of them are as powerful as the gods he just beat and made fools of. To solidify this, Ji voices a challenge to make sure his path will be unimpeded.

"Anyone else?" He asks threateningly. The remaining gods back down as he predicted they would. "Thought so." He says as he makes his way to the Creator.

CHAPTER SEVENTEEN

With the gods no longer in his way, Ji reaches the Creator's realm nigh instantly. His realm is much the same as the gods' realms, with the exception of the ground itself being paved in gold and the walls appearing as some kind of cascading diamond or equally sparkling-type of substance. As soon as Ji steps foot in the realm, he is bombarded, surrounded by the Creator's Heralds who are powerful beings of light, unable to be comprehended by mere mortal minds, just like the gods. Just like the gods, their very presence drives humans insane and overwhelms the limits of the human mind, and like he did against the gods, Ji merely steals the limits of his mind and his perception, and sees them just find.

"So...are you guys my welcoming party then?" He asks in a serious tone, half joking as he looks around at the true form of the Creator's Heralds. The heralds are...strange in appearance once one is able to perceive them. Some look monstrous such as a wheel made of thousands of glowing eyes, looking everywhere and everywhen at once, or a dragon with three heads and many tails that seems more like an advanced monster one would fight in a fantasy tale or video game. Others were more humanoid, looking like a normal mortal man, albeit with a divine glow. The rest were a combination of the two, humanoid men with features that made them into monsters such as having a stone face or many wings, or multiple heads and arms. Regardless of their appearance, Ji is not shook and speaks again.

"Take me to the Creator." He commands with authority. The heralds respond in form of attack, sending their light at Ji in an attempt to pulverize his essence from this world. Like the attacks of the gods, Ji has already stolen enough things from himself that the attack does nothing and causes no pain. Ji shrugs at the attempt and addresses them once more. "I'll let that one go as a mistake. Now take me to him." He demands once more. This time the heralds reply both in voice and attack, their voice having the divine tinge to it, but also a strange echo or resonating factor that isn't present in the gods' voices.

"Never!"

"You shall not pass!"

"Mortal eyes shall not lie upon the Creator!"

Comes the cries of multiple heralds, all staunch in their support for their creator and not letting Ji past. As they cry out, they also attack with their light once more, each with different effects. Some try to snuff him out of existence, others try to rip his very essence apart, a few try to deconstruct him, and several try to warp everything around him to get rid of him. Again, none of the attacks work due to Ji's self-thievery. Ji stares back at them with a bored look.

"Are you done? You can't harm me. Just take me to the Creator before I lose patience." He states in an irritated tone. The heralds don't listen and attack once more, this time aiming for his mind as they show him the reality of creation, the hidden truths of the universe, the whispers of the Ether, all that will make a human mind go insane with just a threat of contact; but as said before Ji stole the limits to his mind and the ability to go insane, so the mental attacks are rendered useless. Seeing that they won't listen to him, Ji doesn't bother with more words and instead reaches out and snatches their light. As a result, the Creators Heralds, a nigh infinite number of beings, are snuffed out just like that. With a sigh and a shake of his head, he moves forward to find his destination, having also stolen the information from the heralds' minds.

It doesn't take long for Ji to come before the Creator, meeting him face to face as he sits on a throne of what appears to be some kind of black diamond or gem. The Creator is a god of gods, simultaneously as large as the universe, as all of creation, and yet the size of a mere man as he stands before Ji. His power is easily felt, much greater than even the god of power, and his divine essence encompasses all who Ji met before him. His form too is incomprehensible by the human mind, but unlike others, it has layers to it that also render it incomprehensible to the heralds' minds, and even the other gods themselves. Ji is the only being in existence to perceive the Creator's true form, but he is not as moved by it as he should be, due to the suffering of one Sharia Iwuhaki. Ji looks upon the Creator's form, a dark man with several forms standing before him at once. One has long black locs that act as branches to the tree of life, while the other has a powerful afro that is the very darkness that fills outer space and the rest of the universe. Another is bald with light reflecting off the dome that is the very light that envelops the universe, while another has a high top fade much like Ji himself, that acts as the foundation for all of creation, a pillar of sorts. His facial hair however only has one form: a beard that is long and braided that works as the seams that hold creation together. He foregoes clothing and instead is bathed in pure divine energy, unshaped and raw, that expands over his body. As Ji sees him, the Creator also sees Ji and he is not pleased to see a mortal disturb him.

"Who dares?" Asks the Creator in a voice that resonates throughout all planes of existence, throughout all of reality and back again. Ji is determined however and thus unaffected by the power or the reach of the voice.

"I do. Ohiji Olezuo, Mercury, the Greatest Thief in the Universe." He exclaims with confidence as he stares down the god of gods in his eyes. "But you know that already." He says, beginning another statement. "I know that you know a lot of things, the situation and reason I'm here being one of them. What I need is very simple; I need you to help fix it since it's the gods' fault in the first place. That is all I want."

"How do you know, that I know?" Asks the Creator cryptically.

"Because you're the Creator for one. Also, I stole all knowledge of you from the gods and the heralds you created." Answers Ji with a shrug.

"And how do you hide this from me?" Questions the Creator God, unable to read Ji's mind as he can all other things in creation. Ji shrugs once more.

"I stole it." He answers nonchalantly.

"So if you can steal all of this, can you not steal whatever ails your love?" Points out the god of creation.

"Yes, I can. But I promised her that I would *never* steal from her without her permission, without asking, and I can't exactly ask right now. It's because of that, that I need you. All I need is for someone to heal her enough to at least come to, so I can question her. And I was told that you are the only one who can do this." Explains Ji.

"That is true, but I refuse." States the Creation God. **"Mortals die for a reason, to my design. While I did not design this...debacle specifically or exactly, it is not something I get involved in."** Ji's eyes harden at this statement. **"Conquering the gods, even defeating my heralds is one show of power, but to conquer yourself is the essence of power. Only then will you be able to heal Sharia without my assistance."**

"I...overstand." Ji proclaims in understanding. As he makes this statement, Ji reaches out, and steals the Creator's power. As soon as the omnipotent power touches Ji, he gets a feeling much like when he took the powers of the god of power, but multiplied by infinite. However he reigns in the feeling to immediately heal Sharia before letting go of said power.

"Thank you for your compliance." He says to the Creator God as he disappears from his sight, leaving the Creator alone at his throne, seemingly powerless. The Creator nods.

Ji and Sharia both return to their special place in the park as Ji places her body down and unsteals time from around her. Being healed, she begins instantly waking up as her eyes flutter and eventually open. Memories flash of her meeting Ji for the first time in over a year, as well as feelings of happiness and love, as they embrace and he says some romantic words, showing her his stealing skills first hand. Then she remembers pain and blacking out, but nothing specific. 'But how?' She wonders. 'We were in a white hole where nothing can enter.' As she sits up and looks over the area she's in, she notices that said white hole is gone. She looks up and sees Ji's worried face that transforms to one of his dumb grins once he looks at her.

"What—What happened?" She questions, trying to get to the bottom of these mystery events. She knows something big must've occurred for Ji to look so worried. He's usually infallible so for him to express something like that…

"Don't worry about it. I made it right." He says with a smile as he holds her. This causes Sharia to blush heavily. "Make me a happy man Sharia." He whispers a she leans in. She's speechless and can only blush and nod as she too leans. Their lips meet and it seems as if the universe lights up as the two kiss, finally showcasing their love for each other.

Years have passed and now Ji and Sharia are back at their spot in the park. Ji is down on one knee as both of them are seemingly surrounded by nothingness.

"Sharia Iwuhaki, will you marry me?" He asks, holding the very universe itself in his hand. Sharia nods happily as she responds.

"Yes, of course!" She says excitedly as they embrace and kiss. "Wait, if that's what I think it is, what're we standing in?" She asks, confused by the situation. Ji shrugs in response.

"Best not to worry about it." He says with a grin. This causes her to laugh as the two kiss once more.

Another year passes as Ji and Sharia hold their wedding in where else? Their spot in the park. Ji's friends, J.R., Marshon, and Bruce are there, as well as his parents, his cousins, uncles, aunts, and the rest of his family. On her side, Sharia has a few friends from the Keepers and the Keeper Elites, as well as some high school friends and family of her own. Ji waits as he watches Sharia walk up the aisle in a beautiful dress with her hair in curls. Her father escorts her down, as is tradition, and Ji looks to his best man, J.R., to present the ring. J.R. nods and hands the box to Ji, allowing Ji to extract the ring, or the substitution for the ring and place it on Sharia's finger. What was the substitution? Reality itself. As she reaches him and sees the ring on her finger, Sharia knows something is up as she is the elite of the Keeper Elite.

"Ji is that?" She begins to question.

"Shhhh! Don't mention it." He says with a grin and a finger to his lips. Sharia merely shakes her head and smiles at his antics.

More years pass and now Ji is with his two children, two boys ages seven and nine, as he teaches them about his many tales of thievery and about the wonders of stealing.

"Woah!" Exclaims the oldest son.

"You really stole a black hole?" Questions the second son, earning some ire from his older brother.

"Forget that, you stole form the gods?" Asks the eldest, still in shock.

"The universe?" Inquires the younger brother. Ji for his part, just shrugs as if to say 'no big deal'. Though he can't help but to let a small grin adorn his face.

"There's a reason I'm known as the Greatest Thief in the Universe." He answers in a sage-like tone. "One day I might even let you to steal something." The children look confused.

"Daddy why can't we steal something now? You did it." Asks the youngest son.

"Because, your mother hates stealing." Ji replies matter-of-factly.

"So?" Says the eldest, earning a pointed look from his father as well as a light smack on the head.

"Don't just say 'so'. You listen to what your mother wants." Ji scolds his sons, not liking their tone.

"I know that, but why would that make us literally not able to? I mean we can just go out and do something right? You don't have to let us?" Clarifies the oldest son. Ji shakes his head no.

"Not exactly. You see...for your mother I made a *huge* sacrifice. The biggest sacrifice of all." He describes as he moves his hands to show just how big the sacrifice was. "One that is entirely worth it by the way." He adds on as an afterthought.

"What was it?" Asks the youngest son.

"I stole the ability to steal." He explains with a grin. This causes Sharia, formerly Iwuhaki and currently Olezuo to smile as she overhears them from the other room.

The End.

About the Author:

     M.A.N is an aspiring entrepreneur that uses his creative writing and original ideas as an outlet to express his imaginative vision. M.A.N uses his discipline and experiences to provide a world of fun, and at times deep thought for the reader. M.A.N. is also the author of Blade Forged in Darkness: an action-adventure fantasy epic that is unique in its point of view, plot, character progression, and overall experience, He Who Leads: an action-fantasy novel that is a true coming of age story rich in character development, plot, and emotional growth, Run: a suspense-thriller that tackles the issue of racial profiling, while keeping readers on the edge of their seats, and 10 Great Tales of M.A.N.: A group of 10 great short stories that are unique in genre and narrative.

65442081R00078